The Dread They Left Behind

First published in Great Britain in 2023 by Black Shuck Books

Cover design by WHITEspace
from "October Day"
by John Charles Cazin
Courtesy of the Art Institute of Chicago

Set in Caslon by WHITEspace
www.white-space.uk

978-1-913038-81-6

The Dread They Left Behind

by
Gary Fry

BLACK
SHUCK
BOOKS

"Gary Fry engages the legacy of H.P. Lovecraft to tell the story of a family's descent from middle-class comfort to a state utterly horrifying. In the process, Fry evokes such stories as 'The Color Out of Space' and The Case of Charles Dexter Ward. *This is no pastiche, however, as Fry employs Lovecraftian tropes and conceits in order to dramatize his characters' slide into confusion physical, temporal, linguistic, and ultimately moral. What results is a Lovecraftian narrative whose political implications are trenchant and timely. Fry paints with a full palette of emotions: there is horror of the most ghastly sort, but there is also regret, and even guilt. Like Ramsey Campbell before him, Gary Fry demonstrates the continuing strength of the Lovecraftian lineage, to which* The Dread They Left Behind *is a fine addition."*

– John Langan

"Satisfyingly weird and intriguing, rich with distorted perspective, both of time and place. An excellent and original idea, well developed, and with a satisfying payoff. I very much like the synergy of the different reported narratives to form a cohesive and disturbing whole. All splendid stuff."

– John Llewellyn Probert

"I very much enjoyed the slow revelations, the mystery story structure, and how the tale was drip-fed to the narrator. Very Lovecraftian. And it has a great final image."

– Gary McMahon

One

After navigating the motorways from London, I'd found myself in no rush to reach my native town, and had taken the longer, scenic route to the Scottish Borders, cutting through beautiful Northumberland. On a sabbatical from TV work, I was determined to build leisure time into the task of writing my autobiography, documenting the long journey from my modest roots north of the border to becoming one of the UK's best-known media pundits. My return to Scotland was planned to help me recollect my earliest years but would also serve as a break from the bustle of the capital and its busy broadcasting schedules.

The landscape this autumn afternoon, all greens and browns and the twinkling blue of rivers, swept by my stylish Jaguar. The car had been a gift to myself after securing a contract for my own TV show; almost ten years old, its throaty engine ate up the miles between my present location in Northumberland National Park and my destination near the Scottish town of Jedburgh. The rural environment bore only occasional property alongside winding lanes. Trees grew in countless clusters and wildlife flitted between them – rabbits, birds, plodding cattle and sluggish sheep.

It was easy to forget such splendour when caught up in city life. This was the kind of area in which I'd grown up, an only child living with contented parents (father a factory engineer, mother an unapologetic housewife) and enjoying a pleasant if solitary upbringing. Books had been my chief companion, particularly historical material, and high achievement at school and then university (Newcastle, reading political science) had been predictable. A first job with a regional newspaper was followed by a rookie position with a Fleet Street redtop and then many jaunts around the world, reporting on UK foreign policy initiatives. Appearing regularly on national news as a journalist had enhanced my profile, and I was now a household name among those who followed world affairs.

But there were other aspects of my past I was keen to explore during this trip. No single person can offer a definitive version of all the events that constitute a life, but the one to whom they occurred has at least the advantage of having *been there.* And so, in the phenomenon we call celebrity culture, it's wise to establish your own version first, before – if you'll forgive the clichés – some unofficial biographer with an axe to grind performed a hatchet job on you.

While descending into a valley, I tried to avoid deluding myself. I wasn't subject to *that* much media attention. In fact, it was usually me doing the scrutinising, haranguing evasive politicians, or calling to account negligent chief executives. If my centrist politics antagonised both left- and right-leaning peers, I could live with that, as well as friction from the Oxbridge crowd who, I was convinced, believed my success was due to a fashionable regional accent. But this was hardly front-page material, no bitchy bust-up between pop stars or film artistes. I was just a well-known TV pundit with a gift for engaging the public in challenging issues without partisan motivations.

The lane ahead grew narrower, hedges on either side looking overgrown, as if few people ventured here either by transport or on foot. Surely the local authority had a responsibility to ensure that such routes were navigable, but it didn't look as if a chainsaw had been taken to the thicket in years. Way beyond, fields divided by drystone walls resembled squares on a chessboard, though none boasted anything other than grass. Did no trees occupy the area, let alone animals?

As the hedges thinned out, I spotted a house at a distance and suddenly began to feel uneasy. This was more than a psychological reaction, though unpleasant mental sensations escalated as my car cruised towards the property. Physical effects were also involved, including a prompt blurring of vision and distorted hearing. One moment I was surrounded by countryside, my Jaguar purring like some slinky cat; the next I detected a species of buzzing in my skull, resembling static from an untuned radio.

When a sharp righthand bend appeared up ahead, I felt unable to handle my vehicle. Moments later, my head was crammed with childhood memories, of enjoyable days out but also of grievous occasions, including the deaths of grandparents and that of a well-loved dog. All these recollections seemed frustratingly jumbled, as if revisited in nonchronological order. Nevertheless, I tried to focus on my driving.

I concentrated on only one task: manoeuvring the car around the fast-approaching corner. After reaching it, I marshalled all my mental energy and steered deliberately to the right. But only a moment later, my front wheels dropped into a ditch on the *left*, in exactly the opposite direction from where I'd tried moving. The Jag hit the drop with a thud that stalled its engine. I'd been wearing my seatbelt, and although my head was whipped forwards, I was held in my chair, the strap locking against one shoulder.

The silence that followed felt peculiar, as if more of the interference preceding the incident might steal in, occupying my mind the way rebels took some autocrat's palace. For a long minute, my brain churned with activity, as if other events from the past were about to be summoned for scrutiny. But eventually, as my shock diminished, this mental chaos settled down, like a conflagration dowsed in thick foam.

After snapping off my seatbelt, I climbed outside, wondering how much damage the Jaguar had sustained. The engine had refused to restart when I'd tried it; there must be serious issues. Despite my rich understandings of politics and history, I knew nothing about cars; as far as I could ascertain, the problem involved the ignition failing to catch, each turn of the key sending the rev needle soaring, only to fall again, like a brief candle extinguished. I wondered how easily the vehicle might be revived by an able mechanic, even if it could be extracted from its shallow grave.

I was prudent enough to be a member of a breakdown recovery organisation. When I'd owned much worse cars than the Jag, I'd made regular use of such services, which commonly involved some guy in a pickup truck towing the vehicle away, carrying me in the cab beside him. It was another thirty miles north to Jedburgh; if the car couldn't be fixed on the spot, I'd have it taken to a garage in the town to be repaired while I stayed in a hotel.

Still feeling agitated, I made the call on my mobile, offering up the postcode I'd fished from my smartphone. The telephonist told me that I'd be sent a text as soon as the nearest recovery agent was located. I thanked her and hung up. Then I stooped in front of my car, trying to assess how bad things looked down there.

In the ditch beneath my wheels, withered grass grew in rich profusion; the soil was hard and stony, looking unlikely to support other vegetation. But then my attention was drawn to a surprising sight. Were there *mushrooms* here? Various bulbous growths in front of my vehicle resembled a species of fungi, though I was astonished by their size. In contrast to other growths in the area, these stood rather tall, their bloated heads a queer off-white colour which must surely be an effect of shadows from the hedge falling upon them.

Ten minutes had passed since I'd made my call; previous episodes had rarely involved such a lengthy wait for recovery. A little more of my frustration returned – bordering on anger, in fact – and I felt like kicking the car. With my head still reeling from what I'd just experienced, I struggled to control myself. It was true that the breakdown company was one of the UK's largest and had representatives across the country. But I was in a remote area, and it might have proved difficult to locate someone at short notice.

Most of these thoughts were an attempt to prevent myself from dwelling on quite another problem: why, when I'd tried turning *right* around the corner, had I gone *left*? It was as if my body had refused to respond to consciousness, acting in direct opposition to its wish. There'd also been that rapid mental retreat into my past. Perhaps this was unsurprising given my current undertaking (preparing my autobiography), but it had nonetheless felt unsettling, especially as my recollections of events had seemed chaotically nonlinear.

Glancing up, I again saw that house at a distance, just a shadowy shape slumped amid a chessboard of featureless fields. It felt foolish to assume that I'd seen this place before, possibly during a childhood trip, prior to the formation of stable memories. All the same, that was suddenly what I *did* believe. Worse still, I'd just realised in which direction the property lay in relation to my car trapped in that righthand corner.

Over to the *left*.

My phone pinged, announcing an incoming text. I clicked on an automated message to learn that a mechanic would arrive in half-an-hour. And so it had taken the company ten minutes to locate someone situated only a short distance away. The procedure was usually very different, with a communication arriving inside of a minute to reveal that the wait for help would be at least an hour.

Just then, more of that uncharacteristic anger arose in me, especially when I glanced again at all the nearby land, an area seemingly occupied only by that silent property and leeched upon by peculiar mushrooms…

Getting back inside my car to ensure safety, I felt bewildered and unsettled, wondering what, if anything, my observations might mean.

Two

The recovery vehicle arrived twenty minutes later. I still felt out of focus but was capable of functioning normally. I'd recently interviewed the Prime Minister on live TV during a major Parliamentary scandal. What can I say? I just knew how to fake composure.

The guy who emerged from the large vehicle now parked behind mine was several inches shorter than me, about five-foot-six, and considerably balder. I'd hit fifty in the summer, and although this man's wrinkles put him at a similar age, I had the impression that he was a bit younger, that a life involving alcohol and nicotine had taken the shine off his looks. He was dressed in a bib-and-brace outfit whose breast-pocket logo read INVERN MOTORS. I'd heard of the place in which his business was located, a Northumbrian town a few miles short of the Scottish border.

After briefly introducing himself – he was called Alan – he asked for my keys and then tried starting the Jag, which failed to ignite each of the three times he triggered it. Removing the handbrake, he (at a perceptible rush, regularly looking right and left) retreated for his truck and began to suspend a tow rope from its front winch to a metal loop beneath my bumper. Presumably he planned to tug the vehicle out of the ditch and then load it onto the back of his lorry. From previous experience, however, I knew that missed out a stage in the recovery process.

"Aren't you going to lift the bonnet and see if there's anything wrong?" Pointing at my car and telling myself that I didn't indicate that distant building instead, I added, "That's what usually happens, isn't it? Can't vehicles sometimes be patched up, at least for long enough to get their owners to their destinations?"

The mechanic finished linking his rope, keeping his body low, as if by doing so he could – yes, I know it sounds melodramatic to suggest it – keep himself safe from whatever lurked in the area.

"I need to tek it back to me garage," he said eventually, his eyes averted from mine. "I can tell by the sounds it made that you 'ave some sorta component failure. The ignition won't 'old, and ya rev needle's bouncing around. Believe me, that wouldn't 'appen with a minor problem."

Perhaps that was true. But as the guy climbed back inside his cab and proceeded to pull my vehicle from its temporary tomb, I couldn't help thinking that he'd just *lied* to me. In the event, however, I merely looked again at those oddly coloured mushrooms and attempted to avoid further speculation.

Ten minutes later, the Jag was strapped to the back of the truck, and I was in the passenger seat, hugging luggage I'd taken from my boot. We started moving, beyond that sharp bend I'd unsuccessfully tried to negotiate and then along an arrow-straight length of road. The driver didn't say a word, just kept his face forwards. Indeed, as we passed a gateless driveway on the left, he pointedly ignored the sizeable house at the head of it – the one I'd spied earlier, which had felt associated with my peculiar sensations – before barrelling on at speed. That felt dangerous in such a narrow lane, and I had to take hold of a grab-bar inside the cab as we rattled along.

Once we'd travelled about five miles, the quiet outside the truck grew pervasive, even menacing. There were still no signs of wildlife, no birds or country creatures frolicking nearby. No cows, sheep or horses occupied the countless fields, although the land was now reassuringly populated by trees. Feeling impelled to break the silence, I was about to ask whether the mechanic lived locally when he eased on the truck's brakes, causing the vehicle to judder as its speed reduced from fifty to twenty miles per hour. I looked through the windscreen and saw what the man had clearly spotted.

Another guy had appeared, walking a dog in the roadside. He was middle-aged, as slender as me, and dressed in smart-casual clothing: shirt, slacks, shiny shoes. Something about his comportment made me assume that he worked in a professional role, maybe even operating a business from home. Might he be an accountant or some sort of consultant? I'd developed a *nous* about such matters during years spent interacting with people in similar upper-tax-bracket occupations.

It hadn't escaped my notice that Alan the mechanic had failed to recognise me from TV, but that was hardly surprising. Statistics on my show revealed that its audience tended to be middleclass, those concerned about the nation and how it impacted on their family's prospects. A single glance at my driver's third-left finger revealed no wedding ring.

As the truck slowed to a halt close to the pedestrian out with his hound, I wondered two things: what could Alan the tradesman have in common with this refined looking newcomer? And would such a *Guardian*-reading type be familiar with my journalism?

Craving no attention, I slunk down in my seat, using one hand to conceal most of my face. The guy was on the other side of the truck anyway, and when Alan rolled down his window with the kind of manual lever I hadn't seen in maybe twenty years, I listened to what followed.

"Is everything… okay?" asked the pedestrian over the truck's rough idle, and I detected a hesitation in the question, as if something remained unspoken here. I wondered if the dog walker was one of the mechanic's customers and had just referred to engine issues. But that made little sense. In such a scenario, why stop to speak at all? Why not just raise a cheery hand, as if to say, "Bloody cars! Always breaking down!" In short, why ask with a suspicious pause: "Is everything… okay?"

Perhaps I was being a paranoiac, but my observation refused to be dismissed. Still unnoticed by the pedestrian, I attended to the driver's response.

"Yeah, it's fine. I wasn't up there long – twenty minutes max."

Had Alan referred to the length of time it had taken him to load my car onto his pickup vehicle? If so, why would the other guy be interested in such information? More worryingly, if the mechanic had spent only twenty minutes in that valley, how long had *I* been there? After my crash and the wait for recovery, a whole hour perhaps? And what implications might this have for my wellbeing?

I was surely being foolish, but two recollections supported my concerns. The first involved how I'd felt back in that area, so disoriented that I was unable to drive safely. The second concerned those queer-looking mushrooms, each possibly even an inducer of mild hallucinations…

Once the smartly dressed guy had said, "Okay, that's good. Stay well, my friend," the recovery truck moved on, Alan working through its gears as he accelerated. This time he settled at forty miles per hour, a sensible speed in tight country lanes. After five-hundred yards we passed a large residential property – two storeys high, with a gated driveway – and I knew that this would belong to the man with the dog, the one who clearly shared some local secret with my shabby chauffeur.

When we reached a sign for Invern ten minutes later, Alan finally spoke again.

"You know I won't be able to get ya car fixed for a few days, don't you?"

I'd told him earlier that I planned to stay in the area while the repair was dealt with, but now realised that I had no idea where I might find suitable accommodation.

"I guess it'll take as long as it takes," I said, in no real hurry to reach Jedburgh, where I'd rented a holiday cottage for a week and could arrive whenever I pleased. "Can you recommend anywhere decent to stay in the town?"

Alan seemed more than eager to switch our conversation to a hotel called The Miner's Inn, presumably named to honour a local industry no longer practised. Then he lapsed into a renewed silence, one boasting a quality with which I was familiar from many interviews with people in responsible positions. The pause possessed a brittleness, an expectation that others should remain quiet until the speaker was ready to add more. Indeed, less than a minute later, Alan spoke again.

"So... what 'appened to you... up there?" His words were awkward, as if he'd battled with his breathing, trying and failing to appear natural. "I mean, with ya car – the accident. 'Ow did it... well, 'ow did it happen?"

As he'd made such a mess of his enquiry, I took pity on him, quite contrary to how I'd handle anyone in politics conceding similar defensiveness. I told Alan about why I was in the area and how I'd taken a scenic route north. Then I described my experience in that part of the countryside, where the valley boasted that chessboard of uninhabited fields. I didn't mention the vacant house I'd spotted at a distance, nor the mushrooms I'd noticed under my vehicle, but I described the curious mental episode I'd suffered, that period of confusion as well as anger, accompanied by distorted vision and sound. Finally, I explained how, when I'd tried turning right, my car had gone left. It was this final detail that prompted the reaction I'd expected.

As the mechanic pulled up in front of the accommodation he'd mentioned earlier, he turned to look at me, his eyes hooded and strained. During a TV interview, I'd have known that I'd just penetrated to the heart of the matter, but in this situation, it felt cruel to push the guy harder; he appeared deeply troubled.

I signed papers documenting the recovery, adding my contact details. The man promised to be in touch once he'd diagnosed the problem with my vehicle. That was when we parted, me with a head full of unsatisfied enquiries, him with a sense of relief it was possible to detect in his retreating vehicle's sudden acceleration.

Three

The mechanic's recommendation was a good one. The small hotel was pleasant, with a smartly decorated interior, a cosy beer lounge, and, at the rear, a restaurant whose menu looked reassuringly pricey. What the hell, I thought. I was travelling on my publisher's expenses, even though these had always felt like a luxury to me, what with my modest upbringing.

My room on the first floor was at the front of the property, overlooking the town. Invern wasn't large, consisting of a market square flanked by rows of predictable shops: convenience store, Post Office, haberdashery, grocers, bakers, and several others. In the evening's dimming light, I observed all the countryside encircling the area, the way amber might ensnare an insect. Then I closed the curtains, eager to address several issues gnawing at my mind.

The hotel had a strong Wi-Fi reception, but before accessing the Internet on my laptop, I ordered a sandwich via room service and, while eating it, made notes of several thoughts I'd toyed with during my drive from London, all potential inclusions in my autobiography. The more I tried processing these recollections, however, the more elusive they felt, as if some sort of interference had occurred since they'd first come to me. And that was true, of course: the road accident. But why would this have such impact?

Here's an example of what concerned me. While cruising the motorway north, I'd recalled an event that happened when I was eleven or twelve years old. In the 1970s, I'd started attending a high school in Jedburgh, a place that had initially struck me as terrifying. On my first day there, I'd been forced by a boy in a senior year to buy something he'd probably stolen from a local store. He'd threatened to throw me over a wall if I refused. I'm unable to remember what the item was, but I hadn't wanted to part with pocket money for it. And yet what choice had I had? The following week I'd turned up in the playground and dutifully handed over the cash. After thrusting the item my way, the boy had walked off laughing, as if decency was just something that bedevilled other people.

I believe that moments like these, nuclear episodes in life, toughened me up for future encounters, helping me to develop a robust nature which rarely backed down to bullies. As interesting as all this might be in my book, however, it was far from the principal problem here; to reveal that, I need to refer to another childhood episode.

Several years later, I'd confronted that same boy, upending the power relation between us. I'd been out of school at the time, playing on my bike with a bunch of other lads. The bully who'd once forced me to part with money was quite alone. I remember how nervous he'd appeared, detached from the playground's pecking order. The difference here was that he was outnumbered and knew it. Other rules were at play in the streets of a rural town. The boy had no coterie of obedient adherents to call upon. He was *mine*.

Not that any violence occurred; I was far too bookish for that. All the same, I enjoyed watching him pretend to shiver, as if his unease was merely a consequence of the chilly climate that afternoon. I laughed at him, and then, *Zorro*-style, instructed my posse to cycle on, our wheels crackling with the playing cards we'd attached to our mudguards to mimic growling motorbikes.

These experiences were unremarkable, despite being so character-forming. But my point here is quite a different one: in a hotel room so many years later, I believed that the later episode had happened *prior* to the first I described.

And yet how can this be? That didn't make sense at all. The second event, the one involving me triumphing over the thug, *must* have occurred later. How else could that shift in power relations have been achieved?

Despite trying to dismiss the impression, however, I remained convinced that the later episode had taken place when I was maybe eight or nine, a few years *before* I'd suffered that threat in high school. I pictured myself as a smaller boy out cycling with friends, the clothing in which I was dressed more suitable for someone much younger. My companions were also shorter, thinner, more childish in their behaviour. Even the bully looked different in my mind's eye, not so large and menacing, quite unlike what he'd become in the future, when tensions at home (didn't all thugs suffer similar family backgrounds?) would be projected onto his peer group, as if that could right all social wrongs.

Perhaps it was my ageing brain, struggling to recall distant memories. Minor whiplash I'd experienced in my car might even have induced a mild concussion.

I wondered whether this could also compromise spatial orientation – making me mistake right for left, for instance. Could it result in anger, too? Indeed, I still felt agitated, maybe a consequence of persistent confusion. Or was this what all older people experience as their bodies began to fail them?

Perhaps a good night's sleep would re-establish the defaults of nature, like factory-resetting some machine. After I showered and changed, it was ten o'clock, and I retired to bed with my laptop. Before sleep, I usually caught up with national news, but on this occasion, I altered that familiar routine. I was keener to learn anything about the region of Northumberland I'd passed through today. I possessed a postcode to assist with my sleuthing, the one I'd used to summon my saviour in oily rags.

A first search online revealed nothing of significance. There were articles about public activities in the National Park, but little associated with this part of it. And why should there be? It was just a cluster of fields whose nearest residential location was a small town, a place so off-the-track that I'd had the pick of its only hotel's rooms this evening.

I was about to abandon my attempt to identify anything intriguing when I spotted an item that seemed relevant. It was on the fifth page of results generated by my inadequate search terms:

Family dies in fire, August 2012

The bodies of the Conner family, residents of an Invern property originally owned by 18th Century statesman Sir John Torville, were discovered this morning…

I activated the link, and as the page clipped into view, I grew excited. A thumbnail photograph alongside the text was indeed of the house I'd observed earlier today, the one a few hundred yards from the place in which I'd suffered my accident. The website offered a grisly account of how the family – father, mother, two youngish children – had burnt to death, but not, as I'd expected, in their isolated home. Rather, this had occurred in a car deep in Scottish countryside, a considerable distance from that property. That made me wonder why the building had been mentioned at all, but then I realised that, in terms of local interest, the house would be more newsworthy than the family, that the Conners had just happened to own the place at the time of their demise.

Despite feeling troubled, I read on. The cause of vehicular conflagration was unknown but was believed to have involved an engine fault. As intriguing as that was, however, it was rather an aspect of the story's background, almost casually dismissed by the article's author, I was more eager to explore.

Who was Sir John Torville, the original owner of the Conners' secluded home?

History, alas, had been unkind to the man; a brief scouring of the internet failed to turn up significant information. All that one site revealed was that he'd been active in London during the early 1700s, expressing fierce opposition to Enlightenment principles which liberal peers had attempted to establish as social initiatives.

He sounded like a real monster, the kind of power-invested autocrat the world could have done well enough without. I reflected on how much life had changed since those premodern days, listing many worthy movements that had taken hold in society, improving the lives of common people. By contemporary standards, the days of Sir John Torville appeared primitive, even barbaric.

But what had any of that to do with the house I'd spotted today, the one this Knight of the Realm had possibly used as a rural retreat? More to the point, what connection did the man have with the deceased Conner family?

Nothing else on the Internet could illuminate me, and so, extremely tired, I turned in for the night. And only minutes later, unaware of which side of the double bed I occupied, the right or the left, I fell dead to our strange world.

Four

My dreams were unsettled, full of bizarre imagery. In one, I arrived again in Invern to find that it had been turned into a model village, like those I'd often visited as a child, its buildings knee-high yet remarkably detailed. After striding Godlike above the town, I reached a stretch of barren land which boasted a single tiny house. This must be the property I'd located on the Internet and, earlier, in its full-size incarnation. But something was different here, and I promptly realised what. One of those oddly coloured mushrooms had sprouted at its centre, splitting apart the roof as if surging from beneath the property, its roots surely sunk deep…

I awoke gasping, feeling as if I'd just experienced an apocalyptical scene, the world wiped out in a flashfire of horror. But then I noticed daylight at my hotel room's window. I got up and paced across to strip the curtains from the glass, observing what I could outside. Basking in morning brightness was the small town in which I'd stayed the night and where I'd remain until my car was repaired. All the shops and houses were their usual nonalarming sizes. I shook my head with self-ridicule and turned away.

After dressing, I checked my laptop for emails. There was one from a TV producer confirming shooting schedules for my show later this year.

Another was from my housekeeper, asking me to let her know if I happened to decide to return earlier than planned, so that she could buy in provisions. She was a good woman and sometimes made me wonder why I'd never found time for marriage. But the truth was that it had never appealed. I'd like to blame my itinerant lifestyle, but that wouldn't be honest. It went deeper than that, something I'd explore in my forthcoming book.

I paced downstairs for a full English breakfast, sampling the hotel's restaurant for the first time. It consisted of a stylish room boasting ten tables, each separated from the others by a network of chinking walls and discrete alcoves. I imagined much furtive business being conducted here, but who would visit somewhere as remote as Invern to strike such deals?

Sir John Torville had once frequented the area, I reflected. He'd been involved in 18th Century politics, almost certainly using the town as a place of repose, perhaps between dogmatic attempts to stop the country from shifting to a more compassionate type of government. More specifically, he'd owned the house I'd dreamed about overnight, and which – I now realised, having fully awakened – was bugging the hell out of me.

I hadn't expected to hear from the garage until at least the afternoon, and so, after returning to my room to collect a few essentials, I stepped out into the small town. A brief browse around the shops did little to provide me with further knowledge about the district. I paged through local history books in a newsagent's, but all of them focused only on walks and species of wildlife found in the area. I felt reluctant to make enquiries with sales assistants. I had a reputation to uphold, after all, and although nobody had yet recognised me, I wasn't about to reveal an interest in what might turn out to be a local secret or source of collective shame.

Who were the Conners, and what had resulted in their deaths? More to the point, what had this to do with the curious episode I'd experienced close to their former home, when my mind had regressed to an earlier stage in life, mixing up the order in which events had once occurred? Indeed, why had I turned left when I'd tried going right? And why, for a lengthy spell afterwards, had I felt so untypically aggressive?

If I hadn't known myself better, I might have assumed that *I* was at fault, suffering a breakdown induced by overwork or engaging with too many shady public characters. But nothing could be further from the truth. I felt fine today, all my memories organised in chronological order. When I turned right in the streets, I went right, and the same was true of my movements to the left. I also felt anything but angry, even calm and mellow. In fact, all was, as far as I could tell, back to normal. Nevertheless, I believed that I had a mystery to solve.

It was ten o'clock when I spotted a taxi parked in the high street. I climbed in the passenger seat and turned to observe a young man ostensibly fixated on the singer Rod Stewart. He wore leather pants, a lowcut shirt, and his hair was blond at the tips and dark at the roots. If it wasn't for acne and a high-pitched voice, he might have been a dead ringer, a real contender. Once I'd described the house I'd passed yesterday – not the shunned one in that valley but the other I'd spotted later, almost certainly owned by that man walking his dog – pretend-Rod started driving that way. He didn't speak and nor did I, but that was fine as we had his hero on the stereo chastising dear old Maggie May.

Five minutes later, I was dropped at the gated driveway of that house. After accepting the fare, the taxi driver made a prompt U-turn and jetted off with a rapid shift through his gears. The day before, I might have fancied the man eager to flee, but now I convinced myself that this would be an overreaction. I advanced on the property and knocked at the door.

The homeowner responded only seconds later. He recognised me at once, vindicating the way I'd concealed my face the previous evening inside the recovery vehicle. Realising how odd it must be to have a well-known public figure arrive at your home, I explained my presence in the region – my car breaking down – and was soon sat in the man's lounge, enjoying a glass of juice he'd fetched from his kitchen.

Stephen Hughes admired my work on Parliament and in the business world. The guy was involved in the legal sector and ran a practice from home. From framed photographs on a mantelpiece, it was evident that he was married and had two children, both now adults. I couldn't be sure where his wife was today but his splendid dog – the same bulky Labrador I'd spotted yesterday – wanted petting every one of the five minutes we discussed public affairs. Then I turned back to my specific matter.

"Ah yes," said Stephen, enthusiasm arising from my presence making him speak quite quickly. "Is your car nearby? I can certainly help, perhaps give you a lift into Invern. I know a mechanic, a good guy, who could fix it."

"My… car?" I asked, but then registered the misunderstanding. "Forgive me. When I mentioned having broken down, I didn't mean this morning. It happened yesterday, in a valley about five miles up the road."

The guy's face fell, showing all the wrinkles of his fifty-plus years. My nose for sourcing information rarely at fault, I suddenly knew I'd come to the right place. I'd honed this skill over the years in many challenging situations: during Middle Eastern wars and African coups, along with more proximate horrors such as terrorist attacks in the UK. But what on earth could be so frightful here?

Pushing myself into further enquiry, I told Stephen about the brief research I'd carried out, including the article on the Conner family's deaths a decade earlier, as well as the scant knowledge I'd located about former Knight of the Realm, John Torville. As each piece of information was revealed, my host sat further forwards in his chair. But it was only after I'd described my curious sensations while driving through the area the day before that he visibly weakened.

Moments later, Stephen Hughes – as far as I knew, the owner of the only property close to the derelict house I'd just alluded to – began to talk.

Five

"I have an appointment at one o'clock, so I'll keep this as brief as possible. I'm prepared to tell you the story because I can trust you to be discrete. I know that you have a thorough understanding of the complexities of life, and believe me, by the time I'm finished, you'll need to draw upon every aspect of that.

"I think it started back in spring 2011, when that house in the valley was finally sold. It had been on the market for as long as my family had lived in this area – we moved here in the early 'nineties – and was in dire need of renovation. Then one day that started happening. The weathered "Sale" board in the front plot vanished and workmen arrived, spending a month gutting the place, plastering and whitewashing and Lord knows what else.

"It was a great improvement. I'd found the property an eyesore every time I passed, on my way south to attend client meetings. Anyway, one evening after returning from Newcastle, I noticed a car parked out front and what looked like lights on in the house. Assuming the new occupants had arrived, I decided to call in and say hello.

"I was made most welcome. The owners, Jason Conner and his wife Cheryl, were reserved but pleasant, offering me a drink and hinting at friendship if that was something I'd like. They invited my family and me over for a meal the following weekend, and I accepted at once. I thought my wife – Abigail – would get on with Cheryl, just as I'd got on with Jason. They had children, too: a boy called Sam, who was six at the time, and a girl called Mary, only three. I was sure they'd be suitable company for my own two lads, even though both had many friends in the town.

"I got to know Jason and Cheryl rather well during the next few weeks. Both were university graduates who'd remained in academia during early careers. After coping with what they both termed *the system* for about a decade, their respective parents had died within the space of a year – illnesses in his case, and a road traffic accident in hers – and they'd inherited sizeable estates. And so, after selling up in West Yorkshire, they'd done something that – and I quote verbatim – made them *feel free*. They'd snatched up that house in the valley at a bargain price, leaving aside funds for restorations and enough investments to live on for the foreseeable future.

"Their plan was to reserve part of the building for holidaymakers seeking country breaks. Jason told me that this would provide a supplementary income while he and his wife educated their children from home. During their previous occupations, both had decided that the national curriculum emphasised commercial rather than personal development, and they wished better for their offspring. I couldn't quibble with that, even though Abby and I sent our boys to the local comprehensive school. All the same, there was something fractious about the Conner couple, a combative attitude I intuited from the start. My wife perceived it, too, having got to know Cheryl, just as I'd become fast friends with Jason. Their focus on progressive principles, liberal morality, and egalitarian values seemed a bit... well, *obsessive* to us. I suppose we were mainly concerned about what Sam and Mary, the Conners' son and daughter, might miss out on by not interacting with other youngsters. Learning doesn't only occur in a classroom, after all. It also comes from the rough and tumble of everyday life.

"In light of what happened later, I consider this an important point. But I shouldn't lead you to conclusions. You must make up your own mind about what I have to impart. And so let me turn to the first strange thing that happened in that newly renovated property.

"The Conners had been living in the area for about six months when I got a phone call one Sunday afternoon. I remember where I was at the time, out in the garden raking up leaves ahead of what seemed likely to be a harsh winter. When I answered the call, Jason sounded frantic, as if either he or a member of his family had suffered some injury. But all he'd tell me related to what he'd apparently just found on his land, something he couldn't understand. As I'd been living in the area longer than him, he wondered if I could drive over and – again, let me quote word-for-word here – *look at something most peculiar.*

"Even if I hadn't been a friend, I might have gone to see what the fuss was about. I made excuses to Abby and the boys – we'd planned to go into town that evening to enjoy a meal at The Miner's Inn – and then drove over to the Conners' place, cutting through mud in the roads. Back then it was very different down there. I had to avoid running over at least two rabbits before reaching the place. As I advanced on the house, cows and horses turned to observe, their eyes unblinking. Birds wheeled overhead, like harbingers of – well, forgive my lapse into poetry but it's certainly apposite – of something wicked this way coming.

"When I reached the front yard, I parked alongside the family's Vauxhall estate. There'd usually be another car here, belonging to holidaymakers staying in the part of the house reserved for them. But at this time, it was out of season, and the Conners entertained no guests. On that day, there was only myself and them present… along with whatever Jason had just discovered.

"Shovels and rakes were scattered around the grounds, as well as a wheelbarrow crammed with earth. The building, dating back several centuries, was L-shaped, its main body facing north, with the tourist accommodation jutting out at a right-angle. Impressive trees grew near the main block and a small barn stood opposite them, where tools and whatnot were stored. Out back, the land undulated dramatically, principally because – I'd been told by a local – mining had once occurred here, though what minerals prospectors had sought I had no idea.

"It was in this ground that Jason had been working, digging foundations for a summerhouse to provide additional holiday accommodation. The plan, I'd been told earlier that year, was to sink a septic tank and feed in plumbing and electricity. A 10K investment would pay for itself in as few as five years, and I'd no reason to question the Conners on this matter. They might have some radical ideas about childrearing, but when it came to finance, they were nobody's fools.

"As Jason led me across to this area, his son Sam hurried to join us, the way boys always do with their dads. But then the man turned quite savagely on the youngster, telling him to return to his mother and sister, both of whom stood near the house's entrance, having raised only tentative hands to greet me. Something seemed off-kilter here, especially the way the man had been so short with his lad. That was anathema to what Jason and his wife always said they wanted to teach their children.

"Little Sam put up resistance, stamping in a puddle. He cried and yelled, displaying a boy's usual energies, but his father refused to back down. Revealing the sort of authoritarian attitude he'd once told me he loathed, Jason shouted again at the boy, forcing him to run across to his waiting mother and Mary. I was genuinely shocked. I'd seen neither father nor son behave this way in the past. They'd always got along so well together, a model of mutual respect.

"Anyway, once Cheryl had taken both her children inside, Jason and I stood on the edge of a large hole in that old mining land, looking down at… well, at *something* at the bottom. It was a dim day, the sky packed with grey cloud, and I struggled to see what my friend had unearthed while making room for his septic tank. He suddenly jumped inside the hole, about a yard down, and encouraged me to do the same. Once there, sheltered from the wind that day, my vision cleared and I could perceive more in the shadows, where a heavy scent of earth mixed with pungent minerals clogged my sinuses.

"That was when I spotted a large *hourglass*, about two feet tall and one wide, but so old that much of its wooden frame had been eroded, leaving only its glass chamber full of what looked like a fine blue powder. I couldn't decide whether the substance had always been this colour or had turned that way during its years of interment. Whichever was true, it certainly looked *peculiar*, quite unlike anything I'd seen before.

"Unconcerned about contaminating what might even be an archaeologically significant find, Jason persuaded me to help him lift the hourglass from its tomb of wet clay, which had presumably cradled it over centuries. As we worked, my friend asked me if I were aware of any local history that might shed light on the item.

"I was sorry to disappoint him. Few people I knew in Invern had mentioned this house to me. I'd once heard some older guys in a pub making comments about the many fields around it, but nothing of much significance. In fact, if anyone was likely to know about the area's past, it was Jason and his wife, who had professional experience of conducting research. But the man told me that he knew little about the building, and that, other than commissioning surveys during the purchase, he and his wife had yet to look into its history.

"I said nothing as we carried that badly decayed object into the house. By now the boy was tormenting his sister, and Cheryl was dealing strictly with him. Jason seemed impervious to these developments, rather intoxicated by his discovery, as if... well, as if he were in a trance. Once we'd carried the hourglass through to the lounge, I felt that my journey had been wasted and that perhaps I might be expected to leave now. Let me remind you that this was the same house in which I'd felt so welcome only months earlier. As I prepared to depart, even Cheryl struck me as standoffish, but that was possibly because she still had argumentative children to handle. All the while, her husband stood alone across the room, staring at the thing he and I had pulled out of the earth.

"I don't like to think that I was complicit in what happened later. I mean, I know rationally that I can't be blamed for any of it. All the same, deep down, a small part of me remains unconvinced by such reasoning. I feel *guilty*. I think my whole family does. It's as if we... as if we *failed* the Conners in some way. We should have supported them during the crises that followed, but the shameful fact is that we did nothing. We were frightened and had ourselves to look out for. We all let them down.

"But look, time's getting on and I have that appointment to attend. In any case, the next part of the story involves someone else, someone who, I now realise, you've already met. Indeed, it was *you* in Alan Rodgers' pickup truck when he stopped for a chat with me in the lane last night, wasn't it? Forgive me, I've just figured that out.

"I can give you a lift back into Invern, if you like, maybe drop you at the guy's garage. It's him you need to speak to about what happened to the Conners next. I'll have a quiet word first, tell him who you are, say you can be trusted to listen. He's a bit of a rough diamond, our Alan, but a good guy. And he knew that family nearly as well as I did – as you'll soon discover, by God."

Six

Half-an-hour later, we were back in town, Stephen pulling up his car in front of Invern Motors. Once I'd thanked him for all the intriguing information, he asked for my mobile number, which I was able to provide on a calling card. The man promised to be in touch later that day, after he'd consulted a few other people involved in my newfound preoccupation. Then he got out of the car to speak to Alan the mechanic on my behalf, which I hoped would enable me to learn more about the doomed Conners.

During the five minutes he was gone, I wondered why the guy had chosen to talk to me of all people, someone with the ear of the nation and access to its tittle-tattle media. If there was a sure-fire way of revealing such private material on a wider scale, this was certainly it. But then I recalled the guilt he'd mentioned in relation to the Conner family, how he believed that he and others had let down its members. That was perhaps a plausible explanation for Stephen's confessional urge. I might serve as an external evaluator, equipped with the capacity to make sense of what these people (Stephen Hughes, Alan Rodgers, and how many others?) had done while handling such a challenging situation.

I couldn't be sure if these intuitions were correct, but they felt convincing at the time and set my mind at rest. Indeed, when the man re-emerged from Invern Motors, I was suddenly eager to listen to more of the story, acquiring whatever new material the mechanic might relate.

"He's not happy about it," Stephen said after climbing back inside his vehicle, "but he's agreed to tell you the little he knows."

"Thank you," I replied, feeling guilty about putting further pressure on the man, who'd seemed anxious enough the previous evening. That kind of thing never bothered me when dealing with public figures with misdemeanours to answer for, but this was quite different.

"When we next meet – and we will meet again – I'll bring along some documents to help you understand the events even better," Stephen said, glancing at his wristwatch. "I'll also arrange for a few others to speak to you."

Excited by the prospect of further evidence and more informants, I unlatched the passenger-seat door. After climbing out, I turned to the driver and again offered my thanks, before shutting him inside and then watching the car move off.

The moment I stepped into an oily garage, I spotted my beloved Jag parked in one of two bays, its bonnet hoisted like a crocodile's mouth. I wasn't concerned about the cost – after years in the public eye, I was hardly short of money – but wondered how long the repair would take. Despite my sudden interest in the locale's history, I still had contractual obligations to fulfil and would need to get away no later than the day after tomorrow. That meant I'd have to speak as soon as possible to whoever else Stephen Hughes had in mind, maybe over a meal later that day or, if that was too short notice, at lunchtime tomorrow. We could eat at my hotel's restaurant, with all its covert nooks… But I was getting ahead of myself; I first needed to hear from the mechanic.

I guessed that he must be in the office in one corner. I stepped that way, telling myself that if the story I'd come to investigate wasn't immediately alluded to, I could simply ask about the fault with my car. When I reached the closed door, I gave a rapid knock, prompting a voice from inside, one I recognised, the nigh-on monosyllabic utterances of the man who'd rescued me from the depths of the National Park yesterday.

If, as I'd begun to suspect, that part of the district was somehow tainted, how much courage had Alan summoned to recover my vehicle? Perhaps that had been just business, a way of putting more beer in his belly and smokes in his lungs. Whatever the truth was, I felt grateful, and when I entered the man's office – it consisted of little more than a desk and two chairs, with predictable pictures of half-naked women hanging on the walls – I smiled as warmly as I could and shut us both inside.

"Right," he said as I took a seat opposite him, "before we get down to business – before I tell you what's wrong with ya car – you should know that I've never seen you on TV, so you don't mean nowt to me. But if Mr. Hughes sez you're to be trusted, that's good enough. I don't know all of what 'appened, just bits of it. I'm prepared to reveal what you wanna 'ear, but I'm no narrator, so some of it might come out garbled."

This was quite a speech – certainly longer than what he'd achieved the day before – and I realised how difficult it must have been for him, especially as barely suppressed unease had compromised his voice. Just then, my curiosity about what he might add rose all the higher.

"That's fine," I replied, holding my smile, the way I did while interviewing people on TV, encouraging them to disclose more and more information. "Just tell me what you feel comfortable with, and in whatever way you can."

"I ain't no silver-spoon toff with a private education. I'm only *me*, okay? Good with me 'ands and that's about it. Some folks is just born to do the mucky jobs, I guess."

As he picked grease from beneath his fingernails, I took private issue with his conclusions – first, that people inherited particular aptitudes; and second, his suggestion that "mucky jobs" were worthy of less respect than others in society, where everyone played crucial roles – but it wasn't the time for that kind of analysis. I had to hear more of the story and was now eager to do so.

His speech uncertain and disorganised, my host began to talk.

Seven

In the autumn of 2011, Alan Rodgers, owner of Invern Motors, received a call at his office from someone he'd never heard of. Alan had lived in the area all his life and had assumed that he knew almost everyone here – if not professionally, after fixing their vehicle, then having enjoyed drinks with them in local pubs. But this man, Jason Conner, had, to Alan's knowledge, never been mentioned in the gossip commonly circulating in the town, a small community of about fifteen-hundred people.

Alan supposed that such immunity from cattiness might arise from the guy's residential location, a secluded house seven miles outside Invern, deep in the National Park. He'd heard stories about all the land up there – including some concerning the property's original owner, up to no good whatsoever – but hadn't paid much attention. Folklore and superstition were less appealing to him than cigarettes and alcohol, and if he could get through a day without the problems that hampered most working men's lives, he was happy to keep his mind blank.

That October afternoon, Alan drove his recovery truck into the valley in which the house was located, equipped to assess what his caller had described as an "odd" fault with his car. Alan had been in the vehicle repair business all his life, taking an apprenticeship after leaving school, and then, a decade later, buying a business from the town's one previous mechanic. Unmarried and childless (more through lack of opportunity than choice), his life was relatively straightforward, the only hazard being complications in his job. Newer cars were the worst, what with onboard computers and other gizmos going wrong. Fortunately, few people in the area owned such vehicles, preferring no-frills models which got them out and about during unforgiving winters.

After arriving at the isolated property, he was relieved to spot a Vauxhall estate parked in front. These cars, common as table-salt, he had plenty of experience with and never struggled to find replacement parts for. Whatever "odd" fault its owner had referred to, Alan believed that he'd have it diagnosed in no time.

How wrong he was.

He was greeted in front of the building by the homeowner, a guy in his late thirties dressed in casual garments. After shaking hands, the man introduced himself as Jason Conner and led Alan to his vehicle. Just then, the mechanic thought he spotted a scrawny figure standing at one of the house's windows, but when he glanced that way a second time, shielding sunshine from his eyes, there was nobody there, only a bluish dust clinging to the glass. It must have been strong light on the pane, making grime assume such an unlikely colour. Moments later, he returned his attention to his host.

While unlocking his faulty estate, Jason seemed quite uppity. Alan had made small talk, asking how long the man had lived here and whether he had family, the usual bullshit that got everyone through life without conflict. After mentioning a wife and daughter, Jason appeared keen to discuss his son, who'd apparently "broken something valuable" and was now in the "proverbial doghouse." But that was when the man readdressed his car, starting the engine with fingertips that, Alan observed, had dark blue powder under each nail.

As Jason manoeuvred the Vauxhall into the middle of the parking area, Alan grew uneasy, even though the vehicle's engine sounded healthy and its gear changes clean. Suddenly he realised why. Before the car had been started, the whole area had seemed too quiet. All the fields around the farm, laid out in a chequerboard formation, had struck him as lifeless, with no birdsong, cattle noises, or even rabbits or foxes fretting in hedges. But then these observations were overruled by the idling estate, out of which Jason soon climbed, inviting Alan to get inside.

"*This* is the problem," said the homeowner, his face registering sudden glee, as if maybe he'd even enjoyed disciplining his boy that morning. "Try driving forwards and then back again – simply that. You'll understand what I mean."

Still feeling uncomfortable, Alan paced towards the car. He spotted a few tall trees standing close to the house, and something about them troubled him, too. Even though all were hawthorns, an evergreen species, none had any foliage, their multiple branches dark and spiny against the pale blue sky. That was untrue of others at a distance, however, whose tops were in full leafy splendour.

His unease escalating, Alan climbed inside the car, settling himself behind the steering wheel before depressing the clutch and engaging first gear. After letting out the handbrake, he started to accelerate… and immediately found the vehicle *moving backwards*.

Alan braked, making the Vauxhall skid on shale. Perhaps he'd failed to locate first gear, accidentally slipping the car into reverse. He tried again, this time deliberately positioning the stick. Then he attempted to drive forwards a second time. The car jerked even *further back*, halting not far from the house.

Now he felt disturbed. He'd never encountered anything like this in the job and couldn't begin to figure out what the problem might be. It was, in fact, impossible for it to occur. Restructuring a transmission to invert a vehicle's direction of movement would mean altering countless aspects: gearbox, engine block, driveshafts. None of it made sense.

There was one other thing to try, of course: drop the vehicle into reverse and see in which direction that might take him. Swallowing with some apprehension, Alan promptly gave it a go… and found the estate *moving forwards*.

Just as the owner had claimed over the telephone, the car was seriously odd. After killing the engine and climbing back out, Alan suspected that the man standing only a few yards away might be playing a trick on him. All his life he'd experienced similar treatment from people, many using him as the butt of their humour, mainly because of his slight size. It was just the way the world worked, the old social pecking order, and there was little Alan could do about that, except keep involvement with others to a minimum and get blitzed most weekends in pubs.

"Do you see now?" asked the man, but he didn't sound as if he were joking at all. "Do you understand what the problem is?"

Alan understood it all right but had yet to come up with any potential solution. The only thing he could think of doing was to load the estate onto his pickup truck and take it away for tests, the first of which would involve stripping down its gearbox to learn what crazy alchemy occurred there.

He made this suggestion to Jason, who promptly consented, expressing only concern about how long Alan would need to hold on to the car. The mechanic, unable to think straight, offered a rough estimate, the same period he gave most customers – "A couple of days, mebbe," – and then got busy with his recovery equipment: hoist, hooks, and straps.

Ten minutes later, he was ready to leave, and by this time his companion's family had appeared, each of them standing in the open doorway to their home. They looked… *strange* waiting there, all staring with glassy-eyed expressions. The boy referred to earlier by Jason appeared particularly odd – almost feral, in fact. His tiny face seethed with anger, a sight incongruous with his six or seven years of age. He seemed incapable of keeping his hands still, the left crossing to the right and vice versa with dismaying rapidity.

Alan hurried away to his vehicle, telling Jason that he'd be in touch just as soon as he had any news about the Vauxhall's fault. Then he quickly drove off, refusing to glance into his rear-view mirror until he was at least a mile away, thoroughly out of sight of that house and its absence of reassuring countryside activities.

He struggled to sleep later that night; even half a bottle of scotch failed to assist. And when he reached his garage the following morning, he immediately started work on the Conners' car, delving deep inside to see what was afoot. Just as he'd suspected, however, all was as it should be, and after refitting all the components, he gave the vehicle a test-run around town. The forward gears took him in that direction, and the reverse ones the opposite way. There was nothing at all wrong with it, the engine running as sweetly as anyone could wish.

He called the owner, using standard phrasing in such circumstances: a fault had "failed to manifest", tests had "proved inconclusive", and there'd be a "minimum charge for inspection". That was his usual way of keeping customers satisfied, though it hadn't been his goal on this occasion. Alan was simply glad to be free of the car and hoped never to encounter it again, let alone revisit the owner's creepy property. Indeed, when Jason came in a taxi later that day to collect the vehicle, Alan's wish was mercifully granted.

All the same, it took him nearly a week to eliminate traces of bluish dust from his hands, which he'd perhaps acquired from the Vauxhall's steering wheel. And the mental confusion and mild physical disorientation Alan suffered for some time afterwards, he ascribed to the alcohol he'd imbibed in greater quantities than usual, the better to get him through such an unsettling period.

Eight

By the time the mechanic had delivered his account (the narrative had jerked back and forth as he'd struggled to recall details, making it difficult to follow at times), it was mid-afternoon, and I was sure he must have work to attend to, not least fixing my vehicle. I thanked him for telling me his story, which I'd already begun to relate to the case's history. The car's inverted gearbox had of course reminded me of my own experience close to that secluded house, the way my steering column had seemingly disobeyed a basic command, taking me left instead of right.

Was it true that some curious power still existed in that valley? And had this been invoked by the contents of that excavated hourglass which, to judge by Alan's account, the Conner boy had broken in a childish tantrum, releasing a blue powder with the capacity to negatively affect its surroundings? Finally, if such dark magic did indeed remain in the area, had it rendered the house uninhabitable and all the territory around bereft of life?

These were my speculations after hearing from my first two informants. I recalled the way that, after crashing my car, my mind had struggled to arrange childhood memories in chronological order, a problem that had disappeared the next day, much as the Conners' faulty transmission had righted itself as soon as the estate was taken away from that place. Both phenomena, I reflected, involved something crucial to people: the ability to organise inner experience and to negotiate the external world. Erosion of such fundamental capabilities could, I knew from recent experience, result in frustration, disorientation, and even anger.

The unfolding story was, to say the least, growing disturbing, and when I stood in the mechanic's office, I felt my legs become unsteady. Having taken up enough of Alan Rodgers's working day, I decided to move on, back to my hotel. But before leaving, I asked a question I'd held back.

"By the by, have you figured out what's wrong with *my* car yet?"

We stood in the garage's entrance, Alan having followed me outside. My Jag was nearby, its snout continuing to gape as if awaiting a feed. I imagined that if replacement parts were required, Alan would have ordered them for imminent delivery. I certainly hadn't expected to have the vehicle returned so soon.

Just then, the mechanic confirmed my expectations. "I checked ya steering – there's nowt wrong with it. But in light of what we both now know, that's far from surprising, innit?"

It wasn't a question in need of a response, so I remained silent as the man went on.

"As for the ignition – well, my diagnostic software identified the problem at once. Basically, ya TDC sensor is knackered."

"TDC sensor?" I said, bracing myself for an explanation beyond the ken of even my educated mind. But I hadn't anticipated a shock, adding yet more intrigue to my ongoing investigation.

"That's right, pal," said Alan, before turning away to get on with other essential tasks. "It controls the car's idle rate. That was why ya rev needle was wandering up 'n' down. Without it and other sensors, the crank-'n' camshaft can't function together. Basically, it's to do with the engine's *timing*."

Still reeling a little, I thought about this all the way back to my hotel, how my compromised steering had involved a mangling of *spatial* orientation while the faulty sensor had impacted upon the *temporal* dimension. I wondered if the Conners' car had ever been driven far enough to determine whether movement left and right was affected, as well as forwards and backwards. I'd never know for sure, but just then I was glad of that: my mind was already burdened by too many other restless intuitions.

After reaching my room, I wondered how long I'd need to wait before Stephen Hughes made the call he'd promised, let alone for him pass on the printed materials he'd also mentioned. I hoped this would occur no later than the evening; with so much knowledge incomplete in my mind, I couldn't be confident of getting much sleep overnight.

I went online in the afternoon to see what more I could deduce about the story but had little luck. I unearthed nothing else about the Conner family's demise, burning to death in their car up in Scotland. After learning what I had from the mechanic, however, this event seemed even more troubling. If the Vauxhall had caught fire such a great distance from the house, was it plausible to conclude that whatever still tainted that valley had caused the mechanical problem? Indeed, hadn't the faulty gearbox corrected itself once the car had been driven only a few miles away? I wondered whether the ostensible powers at work near that property had grown stronger as time passed, reaching out to affect the car so far off. Whatever the truth was, why had the family fled their home anyway? What had encouraged them to go north of the border?

On all these matters, the Internet was unable to help. That suggested one of two possibilities: first, the story hadn't been significant enough to attract the attention of national news; or second, it had somehow been hushed up. Given everything I'd learned so far, the latter possibility seemed the more likely, but I was reluctant to settle upon it until equipped with further information – the whole story, I hoped.

And yet still my phone didn't ring.

Next, I trawled for more material about Sir John Torville, that 18th Century statesman who'd been so vehemently opposed to social reforms. After long minutes, I spotted something relevant on a sixth page of search results. It came from an article discussing occult practices in early 1700s London. The subject was a man called Nathan Hunter, a black magician with an interest in (what the author termed) "the destabilisation of reality, along with all who dwelt therein." Among this man's adherents, it was claimed, were a variety of luminaries, including members of the aristocracy, men of letters, and notable statesmen. Sir John Torville was listed as one such person, particularly when the discussion turned to Nathan Hunter's well-documented (in occult circles, at least) belief in the superiority of the upper-classes, how nobility was enshrined at birth – or "pressed into flesh and bone", as this account put it.

I shut down my laptop, feeling decidedly edgy. I'd just located the usual far-right bullshit, legitimising the status of those in power. But I knew that Enlightenment principles – inspired by work from the likes of Locke, Montesquieu, and Rousseau – would soon flourish, challenging such archaic views. And yet what had the *occult* to do with such pernicious nonsense? What role had Torville played in related events, and how (if at all) had his rural retreat in the north of England been involved?

I considered all these issues while dining in the hotel restaurant. I also reflected on the Conners' left-leaning attitudes, how the parents had retreated from society and resolved to educate their children with a homespun liberal-progressive agenda. I compared this to Torville's thunderous right-wing approach, which would have stopped short of burning peasants alive but little else. Then my mind, perhaps rendered vulnerable by a necessarily large glass of wine, couldn't help but entertain a singsong motif:

…left…right…left…right…left…right…

Moments later, I recalled a disturbing phrase from the article I'd found online: *the destabilisation of reality, along with all who dwelt therein.*

And that was when my phone rang.

Nine

We arranged to meet for lunch the following day in The Miner's Inn. By "we" I refer to more than just Stephen Hughes. Someone else was now involved, a doctor who, for possibly the same reason as her inviter, had agreed to be my latest informant.

They arrived together and were shepherded to my table by a waitress. Once I'd risen to greet them, Stephen introduced his companion as Dr. Walker. She was about forty years old, dressed in a smart outfit, and had natural blonde hair cut short. She carried a handbag, which she placed under the table as she sat. Stephen had similarly brought along a briefcase, which also went on the floor at this stage.

After reviewing the menu, we ordered drinks and food. Then we discussed current affairs but not in too much detail. Finally, once our lunches arrived, we turned our attention to the main issue. Only one table nearby was occupied, by an elderly couple who seemed unlikely to seize on any ill-advised comments. I was glad of that, because if what the doctor went on to reveal became widely known, it might shake medical science to its core.

"My first encounter with the Conners," she said, launching into her narrative with professional confidence, "occurred when the mother – Cheryl – came to my surgery with her elder child, Sam. I was familiar with the family, as they'd all registered with the practice back in spring 2011. However, I'd treated them only occasionally, once when the father – Jason – had brought in his daughter Mary, who'd developed a chest infection, and again when Cheryl had visited alone, complaining of ladies' problems I shouldn't discuss even now. Let's just say that none of these visits had anything to do with what happened on this occasion.

"When the boy was brought in to see me, it would have been early winter, several weeks after the events I understand you heard about yesterday from Alan Rodgers. After apparently falling near their home, into a hole in the ground that his father had dug, the boy had banged his head, possibly on a piece of stone embedded in earth. This had inflicted a considerable wound to his left temple. In terms of what happened later, which a policeman will discuss with you this evening…"

I must have looked surprised, because at that moment, Stephen drew my gaze. "I was going to tell you about that once we'd eaten. We're due to visit a guy called Peter Young at his home at six p.m. today. Can you make it?"

I certainly could, was in fact eager to, but I only nodded, the better to return my attention to the doctor, who went on at once.

"As I was saying, in relation to what happened sometime after the event, I was convinced that the boy's injury was caused by something more, shall we say, *deliberate* than falling. But at the time I had no reason to consider Mrs. Conner and her husband as anything other than responsible parents. So I'll proceed for the moment with that interpretation."

"Please do," I said, and consumed more of my food, even though my appetite was considerably keener for what remained of the story.

The doctor hoisted cutlery, as if to emphasise her next point. "As the wound had already scabbed over, which suggested a few days' healing time, I wondered why Cheryl was only now seeking medical assistance. And that was when she asked her son to say something to me. The boy – his eyes red-raw, as if he'd been crying or perhaps even seething with frustration – didn't respond, just sat in his chair, glancing first at his mother, and then at me, and finally back at Cheryl again. It's no exaggeration to say that he looked as if he wished both of us dead, but after about a minute's delay, he finally acceded to his mother's request.

"What he said was nonsense, words redolent of no language with which I was familiar, and I'd studied a fair few at school and later as an undergraduate. He soon spoke again, and once more the phrases – borderline aggressive – came out mangled. At first, I didn't know what to do, and so I resorted to my usual inspection routine, checking Sam's ear canals and then asking him to open his mouth, which enabled me to examine his throat. All of this was futile, with neither accumulated wax nor tonsilitis likely to result in such an odd symptom."

As the doctor paused to eat more of her food, I had a moment to reflect. Her use of the word "odd" had unsettled me, particularly as the mechanic had described the problem with the Conners' car in a similar way. I took a drink and began to feel queasy, as if the disorientation I'd experienced in that valley might be about to return, rearranging my recollections and inducing another fractious mood. But I somehow held myself together, half-reassured by a thin smile from Stephen. Then I listened as the doctor continued.

"Other than traces of a certain blue substance in the boy's ear canals and mouth – this was neither bruising nor discolouration of tissue, rather a kind of dust which, at the time, I suspected might be powdered paint – I found nothing wrong with Sam. But the moment I returned to my desk he issued more of those words… and that was when something occurred to me."

The doctor stared my way. I gazed back unblinking, the implacable method I'd developed while dealing with headstrong politicians oh-so-certain of their convictions. But my latest informant wasn't being contentious. In truth she looked disturbed by what she was about to add.

"I'd recalled a bunch of student friends back at university, particularly a game they'd often played in the evenings. Some had learned to *speak backwards* and playfully competed in terms of who could sustain the longest passage without error. I and a few others often listened to them, and when alcohol kicked in it got funnier. But years later, in quite a different context, the same thing didn't seem so frivolous anymore.

"I grabbed a digital recorder from inside my desk and then asked the boy to speak again. I was convinced that, as far as he was concerned, he communicated the way he always had, which perhaps accounted for his agitation, as nobody was able to understand him. His mother held one of his arms, but Sam kept throwing her off, as if he had behavioural difficulties. The Conners didn't strike me as the kind of family to suffer such problems – they were affluent and educated – but I'd heard that their son didn't attend the town school and that there were no plans to send the younger daughter there, either."

After setting aside her cutlery, the doctor reached beneath the table, accessing the handbag with which I'd seen her arrive. She straightened up, holding a device that resembled a mobile phone but which was narrower and fatter. I'd used similar gadgets in my own work; they required no cumbersome cassette or minidisc for storage, permitting instant manipulation of sound.

"Please listen to this," said the doctor, pressing a button on one side of the digital recorder.

Stephen and I, putting down our own cutlery, obeyed. The restaurant was still quiet, just a few besuited men with perhaps a similar need for privacy now seated near the entrance. The recording's playback volume was loud enough for only us to hear, though I couldn't even have begun to transcribe what I heard from the speakers.

It was the voice of a boy, perhaps six or seven years old, but surely no other youth had ever uttered such bizarre speech. The multiple syllables, if that was how these fragments of sound could be described, were distorted, as if too many consonants or vowels were clustered together. If I hadn't known better, I might have considered the child brain-damaged.

Once the recording ended, the doctor glanced at me. I assumed that Stephen had heard it previously but, with intrigue and disquiet coursing through me, I was unable to look at him. Then the doctor spoke again.

"Cheryl had become agitated, this sudden reminder of her son's problem clearly upsetting her all the more. That forced me to act quickly. I downloaded the file to my desktop computer and opened it with a media application. Then I played the recording – but this time *backwards*."

The doctor brandished her digital device, activating a second file. On this occasion, the language used was familiar English, just a boy speaking clearly. All the same, his comments deeply disturbed me.

"*I broke the object from the hole outside and Daddy's shouted at me ever since,*" said the voice, more than a decade after these words had first been uttered. "*Now it's doing nasty things to everything around us.*"

Both declarations were shocking, not least because they supported conclusions that I'd drawn from all I'd learned so far about the Conner family. It was also troubling to reflect that this otherwise healthy boy had, after sustaining a mere blow to the head, started talking backwards, as if the space-time issues that had once compromised the family's vehicle, along with territory around their home, were now getting to work on *people*.

When the doctor spoke again, I paid rapt attention.

"Cheryl was clearly alarmed by these developments, particularly her son's accusation against his dad. Indeed, that was when she dragged the boy off his seat, delivering a swift slap to his head. Before exiting the room with Sam in tow, she turned and nodded at my computer, as if to suggest that if what I'd just witnessed became known to authorities, I'd be sued for breach of medical privacy.

"And what could I do? Unless in possession of incontestable evidence of a child being mistreated, I had no grounds to report a suspected case. Was a minor head injury enough to support my belief that violence had occurred? Confused and upset by what

I'd just experienced, I very much doubted it at the time.

"During the next few weeks, I remained mindful of activities up at the Conners' place, asking people in the town whether they'd seen or heard from the family. But at that early stage of my career, I was always busy, with countless meetings to attend at nearby hospitals and care trusts. And however strange that consultation had been, it inevitably got pushed to the back of my mind."

There was a pause, during which we all remained silent. Then the doctor smiled awkwardly and went on.

"Anyway, I think it's time for Stephen to take over. After all, that's why the two of us agreed to come today: we *both* have more to add."

I turned to the man, wondering what he might be about to say. And after drawing in a lengthy breath, he satisfied my fearful curiosity.

Ten

Stephen Hughes's friendship with Jason, which had quickly developed after the Conners had moved to the area, faltered after that episode involving discovery of the hourglass. Time had passed, and Stephen's work (as well as that of his wife Abigail, an academic who regularly commuted to Glasgow) had provided an excuse to keep distance between the two families. The truth was that Stephen suspected something profoundly amiss at the house mere miles from his own home, and he didn't want to endanger his loved ones.

His concerns only deepened while driving past the Conners' house soon after Christmas of 2011. The Northumbrian countryside was barren at the best of times but in winter it was almost desolate, with no animals in the snow-covered fields and most vegetation lacking colour and form. On this occasion, it was the trees in particular that Stephen noticed alongside that L-shaped building: they all looked shorter. Slowing his vehicle, he observed that these fine hawthorns, once dominant in the landscape, had lost their stature, making the house appear newly prominent.

Unable to dismiss his worries, Stephen decided a week later to pay the Conners another visit. It was January of 2012 and frost had yet to lessen its grip on the National Park, the roads feeling slippery under his car's wheels. All the same, he and Jack, his elder son, reached their neighbours' home and parked alongside the family's Vauxhall, whose tyres looked so flat it surely couldn't have been used in a while. No other vehicles were in the property's grounds, probably because few people were likely to holiday at this time of the year.

Stephen and Jack advanced on the house, the elder struggling not to examine those hawthorns, which now looked even smaller. Moments later, Stephen had been about to knock at the front door when he spotted Jason pacing away from the hole out of which they'd both once pulled the hourglass. The homeowner appeared stern, as if he'd been interrupted while engaged in some essential task, but once he reached his visitors his face lapsed into what resembled a smile, however pained it looked, like that of a man overworked or suffering extreme stress.

During a brief friendly discussion, it became apparent that Jason couldn't recall when his friend and neighbour had last called at the house. The man kept referring to events that had occurred earlier in the year – a birthday party for his daughter Mary in March, a barbecue in June, a game of cricket between the families in August – and seemed to have little recollection of subsequently discovering that buried artefact.

Soon after Stephen enquired how Jason was getting on with his summerhouse, the boy Sam turned up, skulking watchfully, his eyes like coals in a fire-grate. He looked tired, or worse, but Stephen, despite feeling wary, let his son cross to the lad. Jack had friends in the town, but few visited their home. Stephen had once considered it healthy for the two boys to keep in touch, especially as Sam was being home-schooled and would see even fewer children than Jack did.

Once the two of them had run off to play, Jason led Stephen towards that same hole, beyond a pile of materials that looked as if they'd just been delivered. There were rolls of a thick, white, foamy substance, the kind perhaps used to soundproof rooms. In his present company, however, Stephen found it difficult not to think of the padding that layered the walls of asylum cells. The man had certainly changed since Stephen had got to know him a year ago, seeming far more edgy and irritable.

Perhaps Jason simply hadn't wanted to reveal what he'd been doing where the land bore scars of former mining activities. All the same, Stephen was able to glance inside the hole, noticing that the excavation had now gone deeper, its bottom lost in shadow. There might have been a trace of something blue down there, but this could as easily have been his vision struggling to adjust to the darkness.

He and Jason talked some more, discussing topics ranging from sport to finance to politics. Before long, Stephen started to feel uncomfortable, especially when, for a second time, his friend muddled up recent events reported in the media, as if one story had occurred prior to another when in fact the opposite was true. More worryingly, after referring to a variety of small-c conservative people who'd criticised socialist policies or gay marriage or the prevalence of feminist ideas in modern society, Jason had spoken with uncharacteristic aggression. "They should be imprisoned for hate speech! Hell, just *kill 'em!*" he said in a voice that hardly resembled his own, sounding both harsh and intolerant. Stephen knew that on most cultural issues the Conners stood to the left, but even so, this newfound militancy seemed anathema to the man's liberal attitudes.

After several more minutes, Jason appeared to grow irritated, as if he wished Stephen would just leave and let him get on with whatever he was up to out here. Standing amid pickaxes and shovels, as well as a wheelbarrow stuffed with dirt he'd presumably pulled out of the hole, the homeowner lifted a hand to wipe his face, and when he dropped it, Stephen noticed a smudge of blue powder on one of his cheeks. Stranger still, some of his words had begun to sound peculiar, as if he occasionally spoke in a different language, but not one Stephen could easily recognise.

Suddenly, there came a piercing shriek. At first, Stephen assumed the noise had come from inside the house, and after glancing beyond that stack of padded material, he noticed a pair of figures standing at a window, one tall and the other short: almost certainly Cheryl and her three-year-old girl, Mary. Was there a *third* presence behind these two? But as Stephen, hearing a second cry of distress from elsewhere, rushed in its direction, he realised what the image was: just reflections of tree branches on the glass, all conspiring to form a scrawny shape behind his host's wife and daughter. Nobody else was there.

Stephen quickly located the source of the disturbance; it had come from in front of the house. Jack and Sam had clearly been playing badminton with rackets they must have taken from the storage barn. Jason's boy appeared to have hit Stephen's son, who sat on the floor nursing a wound on his forehead. Bickering boys were hardly a cause for alarm, but something about this scene troubled Stephen. He hurried to his son, helping him off the ground, and then turned to address the other boy, whose racket bore a tell-tale streak of red.

Feeling fiercely protective, Stephen kept hold of Jack's hand and then looked again at the house. By this time Jason had arrived, and behind him – having moved elsewhere inside the property, presumably to continue observing activities outside – Cheryl and her daughter now stood at a different window. But on this occasion, they were undoubtedly accompanied by *another figure*.

Having dismissed a similar image earlier as a reflection of trees, Stephen was unable to do so now, because those compromised hawthorns were well away from the glass. In the absence of holidaymakers, Stephen assumed that the Conners must have elderly parents staying during the holiday period... but then he recalled that all the children's grandparents were dead: illnesses in one set, a road accident in the other. And so who, little more than bones, stood beyond the two females inside the house?

At that moment, Stephen switched his attention back to the male pair of the family, both of whom had come together with identical standoffishness, the boy still holding that red-smeared racket. Growing more unsettled than ever, Stephen guided his injured son back to their car, sensing all the Conner family members watching, watching, watching, watching.

In the driver's seat again, Stephen accelerated away, unmindful of ice under his wheels, simply wishing to put distance between his vehicle and the house. The truth was that he'd begun to feel aggressive. His boy had been assaulted and he'd done nothing about that.

But then, fearful that his mood might affect his ability to drive, he concentrated on the road, suppressing any confusion in his skull.

Once the Conner property was out of sight and he could relax a little – the sensation came slowly, as if he'd struggled to overcome a sudden fever – he turned to his son and asked, "Are you all right, mate?"

Jack fingered his forehead, dabbing the gash there. "I'm okay, Daddy," he said, his voice heartbreakingly fragile, despite his face looking briefly het up, as if he'd willingly return to that house and deal severely with his attacker. Stephen observed this intention in his son's eyes, which reminded him of fights Jack often had with his brother. But then any anger faded as the boy regained control, just as his dad now had. Stephen and his wife had taught Jack how to handle strife without lashing out.

Despite his son's reassurance, Stephen thought Jack's tone had conceded a worry he might be reluctant to express. After pulling the car into a layby, Stephen waited in silence, giving the boy time to gather his thoughts. Less than a minute later, this strategy paid off.

"Something's wrong with Sam, Daddy," Jack said, his words tremulous but spoken with commendable concern. "I couldn't tell what it was when we started to play badminton, but then I realised. For one thing, he kept speaking in a funny accent – no, I mean the other thing... what is it? Oh yeah, in a different language."

Stephen stiffened, his limbs feeling so suddenly cold that he had to turn up the dashboard heater. Remembering how the elder Conner had also mangled particular words, he drew breath and asked, "What do you mean, Jack?"

"It was weird. Like those silly creatures on TV that Luke loves," – Luke was Jack's younger brother, five years old and full of life – "but *much* scarier."

"Okay, okay," said Stephen, eager not to alarm his boy. Then, despite not believing it for a moment, he summoned a rational explanation for what his son had observed. "Maybe Sam's parents are teaching him how to speak a foreign language. That can sound funny sometimes, just like you said."

Perhaps Jack had detected uncertainty in his father's voice, because that was when he added, "That wasn't the only thing, Daddy."

Stephen, unable to think of anything else to say, braced himself for impact. "Go on," he said, reaching across to hold one of the boy's hands.

"I didn't get it for a while but then remembered," Jack went on, his eyes widening with renewed disquiet. "There's a boy in my class who's the same, whenever we do games at school. It's harder playing against them, Daddy. You have to take your shots differently."

"What do you mean? I don't understand. It's harder playing against *who*?"

"Against people who are *left-handed*, Daddy," the boy explained, waving his free arm on that side to emphasise the point. "When I played badminton with Sam last year, he wasn't like that. He held his racket in his right hand. But he doesn't do that anymore. Now he uses the *other*."

Eleven

"Much of this confirmed what I'd come to believe about Jason and Cheryl Conner," said Stephen, his articulate account of events that had occurred a decade earlier ending as our meals did. "Their progressive values were morally worthy only on the surface. Dig a bit deeper and their true characters were revealed. It wasn't merely the fact that, by home-schooling the children, they'd taken them away from the world at large and all it can teach. I also felt that, first among the parents and later the kids, there was a *disgust* with that world, which flipped over all too easily into intolerance. I guess I mean that I'd sensed the *hatred* that existed in all their hearts, possibly even after first meeting them. And maybe, just maybe, what happened in their new home, all the weird stuff we've described to you, *exposed* rather than created that."

The man might have observed my alarmed reaction when he'd used the word "hatred," because he went quickly on.

"I'm afraid we'll have to wait until later to discuss what remains of the story. I have a feeling that our friend here must leave."

It was true: the doctor had climbed from her seat, holding the handbag with which she'd arrived.

"Forgive me, gentlemen. I had just an hour free from the surgery," she said, smiling as warmly as she could, given all she'd related. Maybe she also felt guilty about having done so little to prevent the tragedy that had befallen her patients. Perhaps this was even why she'd agreed to talk to me. Whatever the truth was, I was grateful for her contribution and stood to shake her hand.

"I'm very pleased you were willing to meet me," I said, my head churning with all the new information she'd provided. "I assure you that everything you've said will go no further."

"That would be appreciated," she replied with another smile, but when she glanced at Stephen, she looked unconvinced by my promise. Moments later, however, she simply headed for the exit.

Then there was only Stephen Hughes and me, the way all this had begun. When I sat and looked again at my companion, I observed that, much like the doctor earlier, he'd just removed something from the briefcase he'd brought along. It was a cardboard folder containing what appeared to be a number of documents. Offering me only a brief glimpse of the first few pages, he snapped shut the file and handed it across.

"After my last visit to the Conners' home I wasted no time in researching the place, seeking information from a variety of sources. And those…" – he pointed at the folder in front of me – "…are the results."

I wasn't sure how to respond; equal parts excitement and unease seemed to have robbed me of words. That at least allowed Stephen to add more.

"I should warn you that it's all extremely bizarre. I just wish that I'd acted upon these facts at the time. But I had no way of knowing what would happen later. All I possessed were diffuse observations – the shrunken trees, the boy's peculiar behaviour, whatever his father had mined beneath his grounds – and now *this* material." Dropping one hand on the folder, he tried and yet failed to smile. "Before I pick you up later and take you to meet our final informant, you should read all about it."

I was certainly eager to do so. Indeed, after arranging a time at which to meet that evening, Stephen departed, leaving me free to retreat upstairs for some essential privacy.

Twelve

It was two o'clock by the time I was safely locked in my room, a kettle close at hand to ensure a constant supply of coffee. After kicking off my shoes and laying on the bed, I opened the folder Stephen had given me. I had four hours to read through the material and considered that manageable. There were around thirty sheets, some stapled to form lengthy documents, the rest single pages providing additional information. Here were photocopies, word-processor files, printed webpages, and even original photographs. I made a prompt start.

Most of the material related to that notorious 18th century statesman Sir John Torville, who'd principally resided in London but often ventured north whenever he was in need of rural solace. And yet was there more to these visits, a specific reason he'd selected Invern, a small town in the depths of what was now called Northumberland National Park?

One document suggested that was so. It focused on a mineral once mined in the north of England, whose ancient landscape had been affected by geological slippages during various stages of the ice age. The substance – the account's author described it as a derivative of ore but added little else – possessed properties believed to have specific application in occult practices. One ritual utilising this mineral apparently disoriented subjects to such a degree that their behaviour became reckless. Its inclusion in other spells was even said to alter whole environments, casting time and space in flux.

I wished I could scoff at such fanciful material, but after all I'd learned lately, I found that impossible. Setting aside the document, I read on, but evidence presented in the next item was no more reassuring. Here was a detailed account of Sir John Torville's involvement with the practitioner of dark arts I recalled from my own scant research: Nathan Hunter. This man, along with Torville and other dishonourable luminaries of the era (circa 1710-25), had taken vehement exception to celebrated thinkers, including philosophers, economists, fiction writers, and what we describe today as sociocultural commentators but back then were referred to as essayists. The main issue this elite group had raised with such enlightened newcomers concerned people's potential for upward mobility, the way anyone, even if born savage, could, with an appropriate upbringing, develop abilities previously considered the exclusive domain of inherited dispositions, of character communicated only by blood.

I knew much of this history, having studied the issues as an undergraduate. I reflected on the Enlightenment period, in which this type of thinking had taken grip of the Western world, as the centre of intellectual gravity had moved from religious faith towards science and reason. This would have presented difficulties for all the educated traditionalists with whom Torville fraternised. The prospect of the lower classes gaining even a slice of their wealth and power would hardly have filled such aristocratic types with yearnings for reform; they'd have been firmly against these radical ideas.

I'd got through ten of the documents, each offering a fresh understanding of the unfolding story. Then I chanced upon a set of articles that, unlike the others, appeared to be composed of original text, almost certainly diary extracts or verbatim transcriptions from public speeches. The author was Sir John Torville, and here I cite some of the more revealing passages.

> *Journeyed from London once more – a hell of a ride! But I am assured that the trip will be worth every unpleasant second I spent in that confounded carriage… The north remains as cold and unwelcoming as ever, peasants in the town making few efforts to ease my progress… The house, unoccupied for months, took hours to heat by open fire, but I am now prepared for industry… The substance, much of which I have stored belowground, responds pleasingly to rituals provided by the learned Mr. Hunter… Beginning life inside the laboratory as a grey ash, it turns, upon repeated iterations of forbidden words, a startling blue… Will that make it more difficult to communicate across the capital? I shall have to devise a way of ensuring that this will occur. The poor must <u>not</u> suspect. How else am I likely to achieve the transformation?*

These words certainly hinted at some heinous plot. Drawing on magic rituals provided by his guru Nathan Hunter, Torville had apparently modified a mineral available only in the north, with the intention of transferring it south to unleash upon London's underclass – and yet for what dreadful purpose? After reading more of the man's private words, I was left in little doubt.

I carry out this duty for our kind. People of superior breeding, in both the present and the future, will surely thank me, forgiving even an ignoble lapse into occult practices... And so, my plan: I shall irrationalise our capital city, turning the good-for-nothing poor into terrible creatures of the night. They will fight, rape, pillage, and kill... To ensure that, I shall turn back the clock to a finer time, when nobody talked of rights or questioned privileges, and when everyone knew their place in the world... In short, I plan to split every person I consider a threat to our way of life from side to side and from front to back... I shall destabilise their experiences, rearrange their sense of time, make their left feel like right and their right like left... This will result in a fury, the like of which is experienced only perhaps by the aged, when too exhausted to combat inevitable deficiencies... The undeserving-poor's environments will also be forced to regress, becoming punishingly primal and supportive of no new life...

There was more of this bleating, as if Torville, like many before and after him, was bewitched by his own rhetoric. Several phrases struck me as revealing, especially in relation to the derangement of human experience. Indeed, since my arrival in Invern, hadn't I directly encountered, observed at a distance, or been told about such phenomena? Despite the man's self-aggrandising mania, his words made frightening sense of almost everything I'd learned lately. Torville, a toff fearful of the mob, had plotted to destroy the underclass for good, rendering the "noble savage" proposed by idealist thinkers nothing more than a naïve fantasy. With so much blood in the city's streets after the blue powder had been released there, commoners would surely never be entrusted with new freedoms. Severe compromises to their psychological orientation, as well as to the stability of familiar environments, would inevitably result in extreme violence, a species of unfocused rage with which I was at least partially familiar.

Most of this scared me, but I found one of Torville's statements the most disturbing: "*I will turn back our clock to a finer time.*" Did this relate to something I'd learned earlier that afternoon during the restaurant meal, perhaps an image that had been alluded to? The harder I tried to think, the less my bewildered mind refused to cooperate, and so I addressed what remained of the evidence.

Stephen Hughes had provided several photographs. One was of a painting, a portrait rendered in oils of the monster himself, Sir John Torville. Sporting muttonchop whiskers and a well-fed physique, he struck me as intimidatingly moribund. I held his stare, the way I might do so on TV while interviewing someone powerful, and had to concede that Torville's intensity, locked in time by whichever talented artist had captured him, would have been difficult to field in person.

Other pictures I drew from the folder involved the house in that valley. One, presumably taken by Stephen, showed the property accompanied by the tall hawthorn trees he'd mentioned in his account earlier today. The photo was dated in biro: "February,

2012." The next revealed a similar shot, those trees in identical positions but now *unquestionably smaller*, the tops much closer to the building's roof. The date beneath this one read "March, 2012," a month *later* than the first.

I wanted to believe that Stephen had simply made a mistake with the dates, but as I tucked all the evidence back inside the cardboard folder, I was unable to do so. Time behaved strangely near that house; I could no longer deny that. Laying back on the bed to mull over all I'd just learned, I eventually lapsed into a light snooze, my ageing mind overwhelmed by the prospect of what I might be told next.

Thirteen

I'm not sure how long I slept, maybe as few as twenty minutes – a powernap, as we call them in the media world – but I suffered another unpleasant dream about that blighted valley. On this occasion, there was no diorama village to bestride like an indifferent God, rather a barren landscape occupied by only one thing: the house formerly owned by such a dreadful tyrant. No vegetation or trees could be seen nearby, nor any wildlife. As I approached the property, voices chattered around me – some belonging to children, others to adults – but turning to look, I observed no speakers, only miles and miles of nothingness. Then I glanced back at the building and noticed something pushing out of the top of it. This was another of those mushrooms, which had split the roof at the centre to reach a hundred yards high, filling a moody sky with its toxic-coloured crown…

When I awoke, I was sweating so profusely that I had to take a shower. Some of the impact of my dream was eradicated by the pounding water but certainly not all. For another half-hour I felt disoriented, even entertaining aggressive thoughts. Squarely middle-aged, I was growing used to incremental failings of my body, experiencing difficulties in responding to an ever-challenging environment. I could imagine how people of all ages, previously familiar with effortless engagement in life, might feel if suddenly hampered in their activities. With the brain's bestial core also stoked by chemicals, violence would surely follow, simple as that. It was a frightening notion.

After exiting the bathroom, I observed that folder on my bed and recalled how much I still needed to understand. Stephen Hughes would pick me up at six p.m., offering me an opportunity to learn more. But with so much speculation racing inside me, I didn't relish the wait and simply couldn't sit down. Eventually, as dark gathered at my hotel window, I ventured downstairs, stepped outside, and stood in the roadside. The man showed up bang on time.

We'd left the town centre before I offered Stephen anything other than a tentative hello. I had the folder on my lap, as I'd believed he'd want it returning, and then used it as a way of pursuing all the issues gnawing at me, now more than ever.

"I read everything you provided. Thanks for that. I have to say that I found it very unsettling." I paused, as if wrestling with my psyche, though surely no occult influence still held sway over me; we were, after all, miles from the site featured in my dream. After several seconds, I added, "My only disappointment was that there appeared to be nothing about what happened later. I mean, did Torville eventually achieve what he set out to do?"

Asking such a question, one that subscribed uncritically to a belief in the supernatural, was difficult for me. I'd always been hyperrational, of a materialist mindset, an adherent of Copernicus, Darwin, Freud, and the rest. All the same, it was unquestionable that I'd recently come into contact with Nathan Hunter's dark activities, and in any final analysis the ultimate court of appeal in life was experience, stuff we *feel* and not think. Yes, I believed it – I believed it all now.

Turning into a residential street bearing twin rows of unimposing bungalows, Stephen finally responded.

"You'll understand more, maybe even all of it, once we've heard from Peter Young. He was a policeman in Invern at the time, and was involved in how it ended. And despite a serious indisposition, he's agreed to speak to us."

What "indisposition" might the man suffer? Had Stephen merely referred to Peter Young's advanced age? Had the policeman been close to retirement a decade ago and suffered a decline in health since? I considered it insensitive to ask any of these questions. I'd know soon enough anyway, because my companion had just parked at the head of a cul-de-sac in front of a detached property, whose windows were curtained against the moonlit night.

Before we got out, I gave voice to a question that had bothered me since I'd first met Stephen. "Another thing intrigues me. Why are you all telling me this story? I mean, if none of you raised your concerns when the events first occurred, why speak up now? And to *me* of all people, a journalist with the public's ear?"

Stephen's response was terse yet honest. "Even if you go on to betray our trust, do you think anyone would believe it?"

I smiled archly. "That's a fair point, I suppose. And no, I'm not sure they would." As I grabbed the door handle, I quickly added, "Frankly, I doubt it would do my reputation much good, either."

It was the driver's turn to smile, a weak yet dogged expression. It put us both at ease, which allowed Stephen to add more.

"Seriously, we're all agreed on the matter. We simply felt that it was something we needed to share. I'll say more about that later. I haven't been wholly honest here, but we have no time to go into it right now. So I'm going to ask you to trust me. Can you do that?"

I thought for a moment, wondering what on earth he might refer to. He looked so earnest, however, that I immediately nodded. "Sure. I can do that."

Stephen took the folder from my lap and tossed it into his backseat. "Thanks. Let's go inside, then. We're expected."

Fourteen

The policeman's "indisposition" was more serious than I'd anticipated. He was hideously burned, his face on one side bearing brutal scar tissue, the hair failing to grow above a misshapen ear.

I'd observed this as soon as the man, roughly my own age, had opened his door. With a strained smile, he'd ushered us both inside and then headed into a lounge where the remains of a meal-for-one stood on a coffee table. That alone convinced me that Peter Young was either a bachelor or a widower, and as there were no photographs on display, I leaned towards the former interpretation. That was hardly unusual for an older man; I was in the same position, after all.

Stephen and I sat on a couch opposite the homeowner's armchair. Low light from a lamp in one corner lent our host an uncanny appearance, his uneven flesh looking macabre. Imagining that I was just about to learn how he'd suffered this disfigurement, I settled back to listen to what was presumably the final part of the Conners' history.

"I'm a great admirer of your work on television," our host said, staring my way. "You give those slimy politicians what-for."

The compliment surprised me, not least because its pronouncement had been so awkward. The man's injuries had the effect of tugging aside his mouth, making his words sound as if he were half-drunk. I'd need to concentrate while listening to his account. Once I'd thanked Peter for his kind comment, the room grew uncomfortably silent. That was when Stephen suggested that we make a start, which prompted the former policeman to speak.

<u>*June 6th, 2012*</u>

When a call came on my car radio from the police station, I – Constable Peter Young, the only officer on patrol in Invern at the time – was parked near a school, investigating residents' complaints about minor vandalism caused by children walking home in the afternoons. The officer on the line informed me that a disturbance had occurred at an isolated house outside of town, one owned by a family called the Conners. Somebody staying in holiday accommodation there had witnessed violence committed by one child against another. I imagined that this related to Sam and Mary Conner, both of whom I'd met while visiting the family after they'd first moved into the area. According to the tourist, the elder child – the boy – had put his small sister's head in a vice and taken a hammer to it.

I drove there immediately. After parking beside the Conners' estate vehicle (all of whose tyres were flat) I climbed out and observed that the grounds were littered with building materials, as if the owner had lately conducted major modifications, but none so obvious I could spot them. The surroundings seemed noticeably quiet, with no animals at all in the fields. Despite the early summer, I was struck by the absence of vegetation, only a variety of clustered growths like mushrooms whose colour made my vision blur. While advancing on the house, I spotted a large hole behind the property, where the land dipped and rose. A wheelbarrow beside it appeared full of a blue dust or powder, and I could only assume that the sunshine that day had confused my eyes.

When I reached a barn opposite the house, I noticed the vice inside, the one to which the now absent holidaymaker must have referred. Although it looked at a distance as if it bore streaks of red, I couldn't be sure that this wasn't just paint. The rest of the place held construction items: tools, sticks of timber, and some kind of padded material which had been recently cut, as bits of it lay all over the stone floor.

As I approached the barn to make a closer inspection, I was approached by Jason Conner who'd just exited the house. He looked tired and troubled, his clothing (dark blue overalls) covered in dirt. After exchanging strained pleasantries, I referred to the allegation made by one of his guests. He smiled, as if he knew what this was about and had even expected my visit. He told me that he'd had difficulties with a couple from London staying at the house the last week. They'd complained about everything: lack of gas heating, noise made by the Conner children playing outside (Jason conceded that the pair often fought but no more than other siblings), and even the northern climate. The guests – the kind of people, the homeowner claimed, he and his wife had come here to avoid – had eventually asked for a reduction in their bill. When this was refused, they'd left, clearly planning slanderous vengeance. A call to the police was no surprise.

Gary Fry

I saw no reason to question the man's account. Despite what looked like a bluish substance on his hands and face, he struck me as quite normal, his voice clipped and efficient. His speech had occasionally sounded odd, as if he'd slipped in foreign words, but, perhaps mindful of talking to a mere copper, he'd quickly reverted to English. At another stage he'd seemed to muddle up the order in which events had occurred, but we're all prone to that, and I attached no particular significance.

I remained too far from the vice to determine whether the red on it was indeed just paint. When I followed the homeowner back outside, I observed a thin figure at one of the house's windows, but it was so insubstantial that it must have been a reflection of stunted trees – youngish hawthorns, they resembled – standing alongside the property. After what Jason had told me, I saw no reason to request to enter the house, perhaps to talk to his wife, Cheryl, or to his children, Sam and Mary. All the same, as neither youngster attended the local school and couldn't be inspected for injuries, I made a mental note to observe the family if they ever came into town.

Before leaving, I shook hands with Jason, which proved more difficult than expected as he led with his left and I with my right. It felt unnatural, that handshake, as if his palm were ice-cold. I'd experienced similar only when touching my first corpse, the body of a woman who'd hanged herself years earlier in a local church. I mention this here because it hinted at a creeping concern I soon developed about the Conner family.

I have one more observation to report: later that day I didn't feel well and had to drink scotch to help me sleep. My body grew awkward, and at one stage I became maudlin, as if I wished I were a child again, playing in the countryside around Invern. Before nodding off, I felt deeply frustrated that this part of my life was over.

The man paused, wiping his mouth with a handkerchief. His narration had been neutral and concise, the way I imagined handwritten notes from his former investigations might have sounded. All the same, its content had unsettled and excited me, pulling together information from other accounts I'd been offered.

"This makes sense of many things," I said, turning from the former policeman to Stephen Hughes. "The barren land and shrinking trees… that car out of action… the blue powder dug up in greater quantities… more violent behaviour from the boy… left-handedness spreading to other family members… and the father's words coming out backwards…"

As both men nodded, I realised that something else troubled me about this latest instalment, but I was unable (or maybe unwilling at that stage) to pursue it right now. Did it relate to the figure glimpsed at one of the house's windows, the same thing Stephen had observed during an earlier visit? Whatever the truth was, I pushed it aside, encouraging Peter Young to resume his story.

<u>July 14th, 2012</u>
Another call concerning the Conner family, the second in as many months, reached me in the town centre station. An enquiry had been made by a Mr. Archer from Surrey, whose elderly parents had

failed to return home from a holiday in the north of England. Their last overnight stay had been in Northumberland – more specifically, at the house in that valley outside Invern. I was requested to visit and learn what I could from the property's owners.

I drove there, parking beside that neglected estate vehicle, which now had cobwebs draped across its wingmirrors. On this occasion, another car was beside it – an ageing Ford – and I assumed this belonged to guests staying at the property, maybe even the missing couple. If they'd decided to remain longer in the area, perhaps they'd simply failed to let family know.

Observing nobody in the house's grounds, I knocked at the front door, and soon a woman appeared, one I didn't immediately recognise as Mrs. Conner. Dressed in a smart blouse and skirt, she looked younger than I recalled from the previous year, when she'd been shopping in the town or contributing to social events in the community centre. I hadn't seen her lately, but after inviting me inside, she talked as if no time had passed since our last meeting. All the same, her speech occasionally sounded unnatural, suggesting that at least one word in every sentence belonged to a foreign vocabulary. I wondered whether she and her husband were learning a new language, or teaching their children one. Her eyes appeared strained, too, the irises encircled with a redness that belied the almost wrinkle-free flesh of her face.

When I was steered along a hall passage, a figure emerged from a doorway to the left, what must be a cellar entrance with steps beyond it. The newcomer was Jason Conner, and he held a roll of masking tape. He didn't look well, his face pale and drawn, like that of someone who hadn't seen much sunlight lately. The moment he spotted me, he closed the cellar door with a thump and then moved forcefully past his wife, glaring at her before heading outside.

In the kitchen one of the children sat on the floor and looked so dirty that I had to step up close to determine it was the girl, Mary. She appeared to be gnawing on something inedible from her lap, a black and fragmented substance. Her hair – last year, a healthy brown – looked mousy and in disarray. Her eyes jerked back and forth. Despite her almost vagrant appearance, I observed no evidence of injuries on her skull, which put me at ease about the accusation made by holidaymakers six weeks earlier.

Wondering where the boy might be, I enquired about the Archers' recent stay and failure to return home to Surrey. When I asked whether the car outside belonged to these guests, Cheryl denied it, claiming that the vehicle was owned by a single man staying that week. Apparently, the Archers had left, as planned, a few days earlier. They'd both been very pleasant, Cheryl claimed, even though she'd suspected, after talking to them, that the wife might be seriously ill.

I wondered whether this was why they'd gone missing, some final reckless fling before inevitable oblivion struck. It was a weak explanation at best, but surely the only alternative involved suspecting the Conners of a misdemeanour, and without evidence I was unprepared to go that far.

Satisfied with the responses I'd received, I made to leave, but then detected movement from another room, what must be a lounge at the building's rear. It sounded as if someone were pacing inside, but the footfalls were so soft that I wondered whether the family owned an animal – a large dog, perhaps. The noises struck me as too slight to belong to even a child, maybe the Conners' son listening from behind the closed door.

At that moment, young Mary, no longer chewing on that black substance (which, close up, looked like chunks of burnt pig flesh), scurried across the kitchen floor and bit her mother's ankles, almost drawing blood. I was shocked by this action, the child appearing ferocious, all tooth and snarl. If her mother's language had only occasionally sounded unnatural, the girl's was entirely so, little more than meaningless syllables hissed repeatedly. Then Cheryl stooped to pick up her daughter and carried her towards that doorway.

"Go and play with your granddad," said the woman, opening the door to shove the child behind. She quickly shut her inside, the better to prevent (at least this was my impression) anyone from escaping. A giddy pet I could understand, but if either Jason or his wife had their parents staying over, I wondered why they were kept out of sight.

Before I could make any further enquiries, Cheryl, apologising for not having been more useful, showed me outside. Her husband stood at his barn's entrance, as did his son Sam. They both looked defensive and troubled, covered in what looked like more of the bluish powder I'd noticed during my previous visit. I glanced to my left and again spotted that hole at a distance, nestled amongst uneven land.

A man dressed in hiking gear emerged from the holiday accommodation at the head of the property. He smiled awkwardly, making me realise that he must be the tourist Cheryl had referred to earlier, the owner of the ageing Ford. A pair of binoculars hung around his neck, suggesting an interest in ornithology. He looked confused and ill-at-ease, but that was hardly grounds for suspicion. Perhaps he was simply alarmed by the presence of police.

I bade everyone farewell: Cheryl at the house's entrance looking younger than ever, and the two Conner males now pacing back into that barn, presumably to conduct more renovations. The boy would be helping his father, as sons were always fond of doing. I had myself as a child, but then my dad had died. Fortunately, I'd had a loving grandfather, and that was almost as good – almost, but not quite.

I spent time later thinking about the past, even though my memories shuffled in and out of focus. I went off duty early, because my limbs felt uncoordinated and that frustrated me. Towards the end of the day, I even suspected that if I stayed at work, I might smash something valuable, and deliberately.

As Peter Young's latest account came to an end, I wasted no time before expressing an urgent concern.

"A *granddad*?" Turning to Stephen, I sat forwards on the couch. "But didn't you tell me that both Jason's and Cheryl's parents were *dead*?"

The man looked at me, and then, possibly seeing realisation in my face, he nodded and glanced away.

That was all the confirmation I required, my worst suspicions coming together like a body blow. The trees shrinking, Cheryl looking younger, Sir John Torville's desire to return to a less liberal era: *time had been running backwards in that valley*. All the while, the Conners' recollections of events had become confused and their bodies had suffered inversions, left becoming right and vice versa. Furthermore, the family had turned primal: the son's sustained aggression, the father's punitive political attitudes, the daughter's bestial behaviour, and the mother's hasty dispatch of Mary elsewhere.

And to *whom* had Cheryl delivered the young girl that day? It had been a "granddad" who couldn't exist, suggesting an older man whose movement was so tenuous that his body mightn't even be complete, perhaps to the point of scattering fragments of withered flesh around the house, the kind an unsupervised child might even consume…

Had *this* been Sir John Torville? And had the Conner family, under the influence of dark arts practised centuries earlier near their home, dug up that bluish powder in such great quantities that the world around them had changed, standard vegetation making room for only freakish mushrooms, and all wildlife departing the area?

If that was true, what else had occurred in that place, in that realm of corrupted time, space, and human experience? What had Jason and Sam been working on in the barn, let alone the property's cellar, using newly delivered materials: lengths of timber, rolls of a padded substance, masking tape, and Lord knew what other items? Finally, what had become of the missing couple from Surrey, including the vehicle in which they must have arrived?

I imagined that I was about to receive answers to all these enquiries, in what promised to be – I could tell by the way Peter Young shuffled in his chair, as if preparing to deliver his most troubling material of all – the final evidence I'd hear.

Indeed, that was when the former policeman began talking again, his voice compromised by all the mangled flesh on his face.

August 2nd, 2012

It had been over two weeks since I'd heard anything more about the Conners. During this time I'd spotted only the father, Jason, driving into the town. Although he'd pumped up his car's tyres, there appeared to be something wrong with the engine, as it made an unhealthy noise. When I enquired later in high street stores, I learned that he'd bought a variety of items: pliers, screwdrivers, sewing needles, cigarette lighters, and chilli powder. This was an unusual selection for someone in the tourist trade but hardly grounds for police suspicion.

Soon everything changed, however. The first incontestable hint of misdemeanours up at the Conner house occurred when a car was found in a nearby lake by a man called Neil Franklin, a keen fisherman. He liked to get away at weekends, just himself and his rod, as he described it. But after visiting the police station, he told me that on this occasion his usual relaxing trip had been marred.

We drove out there in my patrol vehicle, to confirm what he'd chanced upon. A car – a Fiat hatchback with a recent numberplate – had been driven or pushed into the lake from a sloped patch of land. I noticed tyre marks in the dirt, though it looked as if someone had tried concealing them with some implement – a common garden rake, perhaps, or maybe just one side of a shoe.

Unable to haul out the vehicle without assistance, I radioed HQ and spoke to a sergeant, who ran a check on the Fiat's numberplate to determine whether this was a police or private recovery matter. I wasn't surprised to learn that the car was registered to a Mr. and Mrs. Archer, an elderly couple from Surrey who'd gone missing a fortnight earlier and whose last location had been the Conner house, mere miles from this small lake.

A specialist team was in the area within hours, including a recovery vehicle, crime scene officers, and a small armed response unit. A serious crime was already suspected – abduction or even murder – and when cops dressed in scuba gear dredged the lake, they found two other cars pushed even deeper underwater.

Whoever had sunk the vehicles – almost certainly the Conners, as my colleagues discovered that each one belonged to other people reported missing, including a lecturer in ornithology from Manchester – had made only haphazard attempts to conceal them. That suggested to me an indifference about being caught, though I couldn't be sure; I was no expert in the field.

But now I was accompanied by such professionals. In the evening, under a blazing sun, senior officials declared that an investigation of the Conners' house should be conducted immediately. We arrived at eight o'clock, making no secret of our approach. After I'd been kitted out with protective garments, I was asked to accompany armed colleagues, as I possessed prior knowledge of the building, especially where danger might arise.

The first thing I noticed was that the car was missing, that Vauxhall estate with a faulty engine. I wondered whether the family, having done their worst to recent guests, had fled the area, denying us their quick arrests. That troubled me. The truth was that I felt guilty. I'd known deep down that something was amiss here and had failed to investigate further. All the same, when I joined a group of uniformed men about to enter the property, I was determined to make amends.

The intense sunshine caused heat-haze to rise off the land, to such a degree that it resembled radioactivity depicted in public-warning films. Strange vegetation had sprouted in many places, including more of those oddly coloured mushrooms, which now looked much larger. Each appeared simultaneously orange and blue, as if the atoms that composed them refused to conform to human perception. Maybe the soil in which they grew had been poisoned.

As we made for the house, I observed that several trees I'd noticed during previous visits had disappeared. I wondered whether Jason, during recent home alterations carried out with his boy, had chopped down those impressive hawthorns. Then I turned my attention to the barn in which the two males had worked. Among welding equipment and bits of pipe, I spotted several tools — pliers, screwdrivers, hammers — which all bore splatters of red. On this occasion I didn't even try to convince myself that it was paint. I simply turned and joined my colleagues about to enter the house.

Nearing the entrance, I noticed that the hole in the ground I'd spotted last time was scattered with more of that blue substance, though the wheelbarrow beside it was empty. Had the excavation been accelerated lately and was it now complete? If so, what had been its purpose? And what had the Conners done to so many of their guests?

More determined than ever, I followed the team inside the property, whose door was unlocked. Indicating the cellar entrance along the hallway, I found myself pointing the wrong way, to my right rather than left. When I tried working out why, my brain refused to assist, offering only random recollections from my past. I pushed all these aside and then examined my companions. None appeared to suffer the same difficulty in maintaining equilibrium, and I wondered whether this was because it was the first time they'd inhaled what might be a toxic substance in the air, which might even have contaminated everything outside.

The possibility was disturbing, making me more eager than ever to move on. The quicker we searched this house, the sooner I could leave the area, before something worse than mere psychological disequilibrium and distortions of spatial perception could befall me.

Even though the kitchen and lounge up ahead, and bedrooms elsewhere, potentially harboured danger, I believed that any trouble we might encounter would come from underneath the building, in the cellar from which I'd seen Jason Conner emerge only a fortnight earlier. He'd looked so furtive at the time that I should have pursued my enquiries, but I could make good this lapse now.

Concentrating intensely, I guided the team towards that narrow doorway.

It was locked, but the brutal application of a battering ram wielded by colleagues overcame that. Then the cellar was exposed... and that was when we heard the screaming.

It filled our heads at once. Turning to observe my companions, I saw their eyes widen just as mine surely had, as if that might relieve our ears of the shrillness. As we descended into the underground room crammed with blackness, the sound grew more intense, thrumming with such power that the dark seemed to pulse and wobble, as if reality was becoming destabilised. Then some fool switched on the light.

It was just a naked bulb on a wire, but as the orb swayed in response to our arrival, it set the scene below crawling with shifting shadows. Amid a collection of laboratory equipment – glass tubes, demijohns, Bunsen burners – five people were seated on chairs, each strapped to the frames by thick rope. All inward facing, they were arranged like the spokes of a pentacle, which put me suddenly in mind of occult practices. I observed thick padded material clamped to each wall, preventing the victims' protests from being overheard outside. Worse still was the quantity of blood in evidence. It ran from their faces and hands, particularly the fingertips, which had, in many cases, had their nails removed. One youngish woman lacked any eyelids and was unable to glance away as we moved towards her. Her irises were red-raw, as if something volatile had been dropped inside – pepper, perhaps. An ageing man beside her, his lip-width expanded by extensions sliced up each *cheek, was most vocal of all, his screams making his tongue waggle like a trapped fish. Another guy – the ornithologist, who I might have once rescued from such a fate – had had masonry nails driven into his ears, surely preventing him from hearing anything at all; red rivulets streaked down his neck, pooling at his shirt collar.*

And still the torture continued. The Conners had rigged up several parting gifts, each operating on different guests. The Archers, the elderly couple whose car had been discovered first, were attached to an electric generator whose needle spiked every few seconds as it administered shocks to alligator-clipped body parts. The youngest pair, surely also holidaymakers, wore vests loaded with razors, so that each time they breathed, the elastic straps grew tighter and tighter, the blades cutting into their bellies. The other man – the only member of this group I'd previously seen – had a box placed around his chest, which leaked in countless places. But the steady drip was of no harmless liquid like water; it was corrosive and hissed as it struck his skin. Assuming this was acid, I looked away, but despite a sulphurous scent of panic and pungent aroma of gore, I could smell his flesh burning.

I needn't explain how quickly we freed all these people from their grisly constraints. My colleagues dealt with that task, as I'd fallen back, utterly horrified. All the same, as the screaming eventually diminished, I felt confident enough to move closer to the horror-show… and then made an even more frightening discovery.

Between that pentacle-arrangement of tortured people stood a vast pile of blue powder, just like the substance I'd spotted outside. There must be a tonne of the stuff here, stacked at the cellar's heart in a mountainous form which filled the place from one padded wall to another. But what lay at the centre of this stack troubled me most of all.

A large hourglass, broken and yet patched up, was pressed into the powdery mountain, resembling a detonating device sunk deep into explosives. Poking out from the top of the device were several identical objects, each redolent of the ear trumpets that deaf people had used in the past, maybe as far back as the 1700s. These had been rammed into the hourglass's snout like straws in a drinking vessel, the other ends pushed into a transparent cylinder full of what resembled gas, but which probably wasn't. This swirling, oddly coloured substance looked too thick, too mobile, too alive. It twisted and churned, to such a degree that I imagined manmade chemicals, the sort found only in nuclear power stations, an incendiary agent so dangerous it must be kept away from the untrustworthy world. And what on earth could it be?

All I know for certain was that as the team finally reached the timing device planted deep in that bed of blue powder, the gassy stuff, aspiring for the top of its chamber, stopped rising the moment the screaming ended, a sound of pain previously drawn into the container and converted to a volatile cocktail by those primitive earpiece–like tubes.

I had a sudden, terrifying sense that some cataclysmic explosion had just been averted.

Fifteen

My car repaired and functioning normally, I left the charming town of Invern the following day, having heard so much from a group of people who'd done their best in difficult circumstances and had since suffered a collective guilt.

The policeman hadn't sustained his facial injuries during the episode at the Conners' house, but rather months later, having suffered a fire in his previous home. In the wake of everything he'd experienced that summer evening, he'd gone out drinking regularly in local pubs with several men, including Alan Rodgers. The mechanic had drunkenly revealed that he'd spoken to his GP, breaking down in her surgery while describing what had happened and how it had affected him. The medic, a Dr. Walker, had been unusually sympathetic, and when she'd got in touch days later asking to meet up and discuss a "particular issue", Alan had invited along Peter Young, who'd made a similar confession to the mechanic about his own troubling experiences. At a private club outside the town, where the doctor had previously disclosed certain matters to another affluent member called Stephen Hughes, the four of them had shared their accounts, trying to make sense of such a disturbing local episode.

It had turned out that Peter Young was aware of something none of the others were: the case had been hushed up by the police. Although many law enforcers had been involved in investigating the Conners' crimes, no information was released to the media, other than a few vague details about the family dying in a freak car fire.

The four witnesses, knowing much better, were frustrated by this development, and, after establishing a full version of events, had sought further facts about the threat the whole country had faced. After conducting research into that house's past, Stephen Hughes had learned what its original owner – Sir John Torville, approximately three-hundred years earlier – had planned to achieve. But the man's plot – to create a powder with such a terrible impact on people and release it in several poverty-stricken regions of 18th Century London – had failed.

Torville had in fact gone missing in unknown circumstances, leading the solicitor to speculate that he might even have died while staying in Northumberland, maybe while out digging in his land. Locals, never keen on the pompous man, could have found his corpse and then buried it, creating an ad hoc grave. That would certainly account for the presence of his body in the area, which had since been reanimated by whatever dark magic lingered there, a residual force only strengthened when Jason Conner had located that hourglass and his errant son had broken it, unleashing some of the toxic blue substance into all the territory around their home.

This was when a new scheme had arisen: not to take the powerful stuff into any city, but to detonate it from the house, using human pain captured in a receptacle as an ignition and sending a huge cloud of dust across the country. That was surely what my two dreams about mushrooms violating the Conners' property had hinted at, especially the second, in which I'd pictured a giant one blotting out the sky, like some nuclear blast. I was reminded of a relatively recent event, when tonnes of ash ejected from an Icelandic volcano had negatively affected most of Europe. This kind of thing happened, and people in-the-know had had every reason to be fearful of similar occurrences.

Whenever the foursome had tried to share their evidence, authorities had refused to acknowledge it. At least two of them had respectable livelihoods to uphold – who'd trust a doctor or legal practitioner expressing such crackpot delusions? – while the other two were too insignificant to attract widescale attention. And so they'd all eventually lapsed into silence, even though guilt ate them up inside. It was at this late stage, prompted by excessive alcohol consumption, that the housefire in which Peter Young had suffered his injuries had happened.

Here is another issue I need to address: what misfortune had befallen the Conner family, who'd fled the scene of their crimes in a vehicle hardly fit for purpose. Indeed, it was a severe mechanical fault that had proved their undoing. As their Vauxhall estate had been driven earlier in the town, Alan Rodgers, still disturbed by his encounter with the car, had heard its unhealthy sound and diagnosed a deep engine problem apt to result in overheating. All the same, the mechanic had claimed that, in a modern vehicle designed with safety in mind, this was unlikely to lead to a serious fire.

But how about a car that no longer functioned like a standard one, which had once gone forwards when it ought to have moved backwards? It had come as no surprise to the four investigators when the Conners' estate had been found burnt out in a Scottish country lane, leading away into barren territory where few people lived, only outsiders and those escaping the harrying bustle of contemporary life.

In any final analysis, wasn't that what the family had always attempted to achieve? My interpretation of their case has been influenced by how the story was related to me, but while considering all the facts, I've drawn on my own experiences and come to agree with an observation once made by Stephen Hughes: the Conners had fled a social world they'd loathed. And so were they much different from Sir John Torville, who'd feared the mob's potential to compromise his upper-class lifestyle? Weren't the Conners' left-leaning attitudes and the statesman's right-wing values fundamentally similar at root – driven by fear and intolerance? In fact, hadn't the family's plot to endanger the whole country been *worse* than Torville's more restricted goal?

The Conners had been easy-pickings for the statesman, who'd yearned for a better time, one uncorrupted by what he'd perceived to be – back in the 1700s, just as Jason and Cheryl surely felt about life in the latter-day – a moral turpitude. In short, they'd all found extreme solutions appealing, and for that reason it was fitting that the family had suffered an identical fate to Torville.

I have one final piece of information to relate. I learned this from Peter Young, who'd acquired it before the case was closed without further investigation by police. At the request of all my informants, I've agreed to draw upon my media reputation by publishing this account in the public domain. Stephen Hughes told me that he'd delayed asking me to help in this way, in fear of me backing off too soon. He'd persuaded the other three to do likewise, allowing them all to first gain my trust. At any rate, I hope this document will persuade certain people in power to inform the nation about the grave danger it recently faced, just how close every one of us in the UK came to oblivion. I hope that the fact I reveal below will drive home the extreme seriousness of the case.

When professionals analysed that burned-out car, they'd found several unrecognisable bodies among its ashes and scorched metal. A pair slumped in the front seats had belonged to an adult male and female, both approximately forty years old. Two others were on either side of the backseat, each that of a child under ten. But it was one in the middle of the rear that disturbed authorities most of all.

After careful examination, including carbon-dating of bones, specialists concluded that it belonged to an adult male of average height and build, and was believed to date back about three-hundred years.

The charred remains of this figure's hands had held those of the youngsters to its left and right.

THE THREE BOOKS
by
Paul StJohn Mackintosh

"I've been told that this is the most elegant thing I've ever written. I can't think how such a dark brew of motifs came together to create that effect. But there's unassuaged longing and nostalgia in here, interwoven with the horror, as well as an unflagging drive towards the final consummation. I still feel more for the story's characters, whether love or loathing, than for any others I've created to date. Tragedy, urban legend, Gothic romance, warped fairy tale of New York: it's all there. And of course, most important of all is the seductive allure of writing and of books – and what that can lead some people to do.

You may not like my answer to the mystery of the third book. But I hope you stay to find out."

Paul StJohn Mackintosh

"Paul StJohn Mackintosh is one of those writers who just seems to quietly get on with the business of producing great fiction... it's an excellent showcase for his obvious talents. His writing, his imagination, his ability to lay out a well-paced and intricate story in only 100 pages is a great testament to his skills."

—This is Horror

BLACK STAR, BLACK SUN
by
Rich Hawkins

"Black Star, Black Sun *is my tribute to Lovecraft, Ramsey Campbell, and the haunted fields of Somerset, where I seemed to spend much of my childhood. It's a story about going home and finding horror there when something beyond human understanding begins to invade our reality. It encompasses broken dreams, old memories, lost loved ones and a fundamentally hostile universe. It's the last song of a dying world before it falls to the Black Star.*"

Rich Hawkins

———•———

"Black Star, Black Sun *possesses a horror energy of sufficient intensity to make readers sit up straight. A descriptive force that shifts from the raw to the nuanced. A ferocious work of macabre imagination and one for readers of Conrad Williams and Gary McMahon.*"
—Adam Nevill, author of *The Ritual*

"*Reading Hawkins' novella is like sitting in front of a guttering open fire. Its glimmerings captivate, hissing with irrepressible life, and then, just when you're most seduced by its warmth, it spits stinging embers your way. This is incendiary fiction. Read at arms' length.*"
—Gary Fry, author of *Conjure House*

blackshuckbooks.co.uk/signature

DEAD LEAVES

by

Andrew David Barker

"*This book is my love letter to the horror genre. It is about what it means to be a horror fan; about how the genre can nurture an adolescent mind; how it can be a positive force in life.*

This book is set during a time when horror films were vilified in the press and in parliament like never before. It is about how being a fan of so-called 'video nasties' made you, in the eyes of the nation, a freak, a weirdo, or worse, someone who could actually be a danger to society.

This book is partly autobiographical, set in a time when Britain seemed to be a war with itself. It is a working class story about hope. All writers, filmmakers, musicians, painters – artists of any kind –were first inspired to create their own work by the guiding light of another's. The first spark that sets them on their way.

This book is about that spark."

Andrew David Barker

"*Whilst Thatcher colluded with the tabloids to distract the public... an urban quest for the ultimate video nasty was unfolding, before the forces of media madness and power drunk politicians destroyed the Holy Grail of gore!*"

—Graham Humphreys, painter of *The Evil Dead* poster

blackshuckbooks.co.uk/signature

THE FINITE
by
Kit Power

"The Finite *started as a dream; an image, really, on the edge of waking. My daughter and I, joining a stream of people walking past our house. We were marching together, and I saw that many of those behind us were sick, and struggling, and then I looked to the horizon and saw the mushroom cloud. I remember a wave of perfect horror and despair washing over me; the sure and certain knowledge that our march was doomed, as were we.*

The image didn't make it into the story, but the feeling did. King instructs us to write about what scares us. In The Finite, *I wrote about the worst thing I can imagine; my own childhood nightmare, resurrected and visited on my kid.*"

Kit Power

———•———

"The Finite *is* Where the Wind Blows *or* Threads *for the 21st century, played out on a tight scale by a father and his young daughter, which only serves to make it all the more heartbreaking.*"

—Priya Sharma, author of *Ormeshadow*

blackshuckbooks.co.uk/signature

RICOCHET
by
Tim Dry

"*With* Ricochet *I wanted to break away from the traditional linear form of storytelling in a novella and instead create a series of seemingly unrelated vignettes. Like the inconsistent chaos of vivid dreams I chose to create stand–alone episodes that vary from being fearful to blackly humorous to the downright bizarre. It's a book that you can dip into at any point but there is an underlying cadence that will carry you along, albeit in a strangely seductive new way.*

Prepare to encounter a diverse collection of characters. Amongst them are gangsters, dead rock stars, psychics, comic strip heroes and villains, asylum inmates, UFOs, occult nazis, parisian ghosts, decaying and depraved royalty and topping the bill a special guest appearance by the Devil himself."

Tim Dry

Reads like the exquisite lovechild of William Burroughs and Philip K. Dick's fiction, with some Ballard thrown in for good measure. Wonderfully imaginative, darkly satirical – this is a must read!

—Paul Kane, author of *Sleeper(s)* and *Ghosts*

ROTH-STEYR
by
Simon Bestwick

"*You never know which ideas will stick in your mind, let alone where they'll go.* Roth-Steyr *began with an interest in the odd designs and names of early automatic pistols, and the decision to use one of them as a story title. What started out as an oddball short piece became a much longer and darker tale about how easily a familiar world can fall apart, how old convictions vanish or change, and why no one should want to live forever.*

It's also about my obsession with history, in particular the chaotic upheavals that plagued the first half of the twentieth century and that are waking up again. Another 'long dark night of the European soul' feels very close today.

So here's the story of Valerie Varden. And her Roth–Steyr."

Simon Bestwick

———•———

"*A slice of pitch–black cosmic pulp, elegant and inventive in all the most emotionally engaging ways.*"

—Gemma Files, author of *In That Endlessness, Our End*

blackshuckbooks.co.uk/signature

A DIFFERENT KIND OF LIGHT
by
Simon Bestwick

"When I first read about the Le Mans Disaster, over twenty years ago, I knew there was a story to tell about the newsreel footage of the aftermath – footage so appalling it was never released. A story about how many of us want to see things we aren't supposed to, even when we insist we don't.

What I didn't know was who would tell that story. Last year I finally realised: two lovers who weren't lovers, in a world that was falling apart. So at long last I wrote their story and followed them into a shadow land of old films, grief, obsession and things worse than death.

You only need open this book, and the film will start to play."

Simon Bestwick

———•———

"Compulsively readable, original and chilling. Simon Bestwick's witty, engaging tone effortlessly and brilliantly amplifies its edge-of-your-seat atmosphere of creeping dread. I'll be sleeping with the lights on."

—Sarah Lotz, author of *The Three*, *Day Four*,
The White Road & *Missing Person*

blackshuckbooks.co.uk/signature

THE INCARNATIONS OF MARIELA PEÑA

by

Steven J Dines

"The Incarnations of Mariela Peña *is unlike anything I have ever written. It started life (pardon the pun) as a zombie tale and very quickly became something else: a story about love and the fictions we tell ourselves.*

During its writing, I felt the ghost of Charles Bukowski looking over my shoulder. I made the conscious decision to not censor either the characters or myself but to write freely and with brutal, sometimes uncomfortable, honesty. I was betrayed by someone I cared deeply for, and like Poet, I had to tell the story, or at least this incarnation of it. A story about how the past refuses to die."

Steven J Dines

———•———

"*Call it literary horror, call it psychological horror, call it a journey into the darkness of the soul. It's all here. As intense and compelling a piece of work as I've read in many a year.*"

—Paul Finch, author of *Kiss of Death* and *Stolen*, and editor of the *Terror Tales* series.

THE DERELICT
by
Neil Williams

"The Derelict *is really a story of two derelicts – the events on the first and their part in the creation of the second.*

With this story I've pretty much nailed my colours to the mast, so to speak. As the tale is intended as a tribute to stories by the likes of William Hope Hodgson or H P Lovecraft (with a passing nod to Coleridge's Ancient Mariner), where some terrible event is related in an unearthed journal or (as is the case here) by a narrator driven to near madness.

The primary influence on the story was the voyage of the Demeter, from Bram Stoker's Dracula, *one of the more compelling episodes of that novel. Here the crew are irrevocably doomed from the moment they set sail. There is never any hope of escape or salvation once the nature of their cargo becomes apparent. This was to be my jumping off point with* The Derelict.

Though I have charted a very different course from the one taken by Stoker, I have tried to remain resolutely true to the spirit of that genre of fiction and the time in which it was set."

Neil Williams

"*Fans of supernatural terror at sea will love* The Derelict. *I certainly did.*"
—Stephen Laws, author of *Ferocity* and *Chasm*

blackshuckbooks.co.uk/signature

AND THE NIGHT DID CLAIM THEM

by

Duncan P Bradshaw

"*The night is a place where the places and people we see during the day are changed. Their properties – especially how we interact and consider them – are altered. But more than that, the night changes us as people. It's a time of day which both hides us away in the shadows and opens us up for reflection. Where we peer up at the stars, made aware of our utter insignificance and wonder, 'what if?' This book takes something that links every single one of us, and tries to illuminate its murky depths, finding things both familiar and alien. It's a story of loss, hope, and redemption; a barely audible whisper within, that even in our darkest hour, there is the promise of the light again.*"

Duncan P Bradshaw

"*A creepy, absorbing novella about loss, regret, and the blackness awaiting us all. Bleak as hell; dark and silky as a pint of Guinness – I loved it.*"

—James Everington, author of *Trying To Be So Quiet* and *The Quarantined City*

blackshuckbooks.co.uk/signature

AZEMAN

OR, THE TESTAMENT OF QUINCEY MORRIS

by

Lisa Moore

"*How much do we really know about Quincey Morris?*

In one of the greatest Grand-Guignol moments of all time, Dracula is caught feeding Mina blood from his own breast while her husband lies helpless on the same bed. In the chaos that follows, Morris runs outside, ostensibly in pursuit. "I could see Quincey Morris run across the lawn," Dr. Seward says, "and hide himself in the shadow of a great yew-tree. It puzzled me to think why he was doing this…" Then the doctor is distracted, and we never do find out.

This story rose up from that one question: Why, in this calamitous moment, did the brave and stalwart Quincey Morris hide behind a tree?"

Lisa Moore

—•—

"*A fresh new take on one of the many enigmas of Dracula – just what is Quincey Morris's story?*"

—Kim Newman, author of the *Anno Dracula* series

blackshuckbooks.co.uk/signature

SHADE OF STILLTHORPE
by
Tim Major

"*It's fair to say that parenthood has dominated my thoughts – and certainly my identity – for the last nine years. While I love my children unconditionally, I'm morbidly fascinated by the idea of parenthood lacking an instinctive bond to counter the difficulties and sacrifices of such a period of life. And I'm afraid of any possible future in which that bond might be weaker.*

Identity is a slippery thing. More than anything, I'm scared of losing it – my own, and those of the people I love. Several of my novels and stories have related to this fear. In Shade of Stillthorpe, *it's quite literal: how would you react if your child was unrecognisable, suddenly, in all respects?*"

Tim Major

A seemingly impossible premise becomes increasingly real in this inventive and heartbreaking tale of loss."

—Lucie McKnight Hardy, author of *Dead Relatives*

"*Parenthood is a forest of emotions, including jealousy, confusion and terror, in* Shade of Stillthorpe. *It's a dark mystery that resonated deeply with me.*"
—Aliya Whiteley, author of *The Loosening Skin*

SORROWMOUTH
by
Simon Avery

"*For a long time Sorrowmouth existed as three or four separate ideas in different notebooks until one day, in a flash of divine inspiration, I recognised the common ground they shared with each other. A man trekking from one roadside memorial to another, in pursuit of grief; Beachy Head and its long dark history of suicide; William Blake and his angelic visions on Peckham Rye; Blake again with The Ghost of a Flea; a monstrous companion, bound by lifes' cruelty...*

As I wrote I discovered these disparate elements were really about me getting to some deeper truth about myself, and about all the people I've known in my life, about the struggles we all have that no one save for loved ones see – alcoholism, dependence, self doubt, grief, mental illness. Sorrowmouth is about the mystery hiding at the heart of all things, making connections in the depths of sorrow, and what you have to sacrifice for a moment of vertigo."

Simon Avery

———•———

"*Sorrowmouth is a story for these dark days. Simon Avery summons the spirit of William Blake in this visionary exploration of the manifestations of our grief and pain.*"
—Priya Sharma, author of *Ormeshadow*

Printed by BoD™in Norderstedt, Germany